Séance at the Lemp

L. Lee Starr

© 2012 Mystic Hippo Media
Publishing

Saint Louis, Missouri

Printed in the United States

Library of Congress Catalog Number: 2011945119
ISBN 978-0-9848694-0-4

Published by:
Mystic Hippo Media Publishing
P.O. Box 350
Cottleville, MO 63338-0350
(636) 922-3593

Email: lois@mystichippo.com
Web: http://www.mystichippo.com

Cover Design by Ariel D. Prettyman

Chapter 1- Seven Years Later

As the midmorning sun smuggled beams of light through an inconspicuous crack behind his blackout curtains, Dr. Joel Russell woke from the slumber on his living room couch. He had done this for the last seven years, spending the night there with no blanket and dressed in the previous day's attire. In fact, he thought, he may have worn the same suit the day prior to that. He had not really kept track. And, as he did every morning for the past seven years, he awoke on his own accord, without the aid of an alarm clock, wake-up call, or the soothing sound of a female voice to gently nudge him into consciousness. It was time to get up, simply because he had slept too long already. He couldn't think of anything he really wanted to do or needed to do that day, but he felt that he should—at the very least—get up and move around.

He was the sole inhabitant of a large estate he had inherited from his wife, the last of a privileged Saint Louis bloodline, now long since dead. In his efforts to cut costs in the operating of this vast estate, (and to also minimize having to inhabit rooms which managed only to help stir up unpleasant memories), Dr. Russell had relocated all his possessions to just three rooms in the home: the living room, where he slept; the bathroom, where he brushed himself off and took an infrequent shower; and the vast kitchen, where he accessed certain staples of survival such as cold cereal, instant coffee, and Ramen noodles. He had initially abandoned the eating of Ramen after college, but since the death of his wife, Elsa, he returned to the tasty noodles out of necessity. He now considered them a form of comfort food—a sort of chicken soup for the lonely and destitute.

Despite appearances, Dr. Joel Russell was far from being a pauper. He had etched out a successful living during the years practicing psychiatry in one of St. Louis's wealthiest neighborhoods. In addition, he had chosen to marry one of Saint Louis's richest socialites. After the passing of Elsa's mother, Joel's mother-in-law, Elsa inherited one of the wealthiest estates in Missouri. After his wife Elsa died, Joel was left with not only the family estate, but the proceeds from a very generous life insurance policy.

This life insurance policy—even after seven years—was still mostly intact. The estate had long been purchased in full, and Joel needed very little to manage its day-to-day operations. He had blocked off unnecessary rooms by means of a Visqueen curtain suspended between the kitchen and the dining area, and he no longer used any of the five bedrooms or numerous baths on the upstairs floor.

Joel rose from the sofa and made his way to the bath. He ran cold water into the antique basin and splashed it on his face with his bare hands. He looked into the mirror to see his worn visage beneath long, gray, and unkempt hair staring back at him.

Dr. Russell was a tall, slender man with a thick brow and sincere, gray eyes separated by a slightly crooked, but very pronounced Roman nose. His lips were thin. On the few occasions when he did smile, he pursed his lips, never allowing his teeth to show. He had a very prominent lower chin. He had neglected his personal hygiene in recent years. Although he was now fifty-five years old, he was still somewhat attractive. But even during his youth, his extreme modesty would always prevent him from ever acknowledging his good looks.

Joel ran his fingers along his chin as he examined himself in the mirror. He decided that he would not shave today. He would settle for the stubble growing on his face, justifying his laziness to himself by believing his growing beard would serve to hide his emerging wrinkles.

He opened the door to his medicine cabinet to expose a bottle of antidepressants. He opened the bottle. There was one pill left. He poured the pill into his hand and swallowed it without water. He threw the empty bottle in the small pool of cold water at the bottom of the basin. He brushed off the lapel to his tweed suit coat, turned, and made his way to the kitchen.

Dr. Russell's cell phone had been charging on the kitchen counter, which was bare, except for a glass bowl of rotten fruit he never managed to get around to eating. *I'd better check my messages*, he thought.

Picking up the phone, he accessed his voice mail messages. As he scrunched up his right shoulder to hold the phone, he rinsed a dirty coffee cup in the sink and opened the microwave to heat up water for instant coffee. He then realized that there was already a cup of water in the microwave still there from the previous day. He closed the door and set the microwave timer for one minute.

He wrestled the phone off his shoulder and punched in his pin code to access his private messages.

"Hey, Joel.... It's Joanna. I wonder if you might have time to stop by the office. There are a few things I need to talk to you about. Listen, I have sessions all day, but I had a cancellation at 2 P.M. this afternoon. Could you come by? If you can't, call me. Thanks."

Dr. Russell hadn't really planned on stopping by the office. In fact, he had not made an appearance at his former practice for about three months. After Elsa died, he had whittled his patient load down to two patients, whom he then managed to unload onto other psychiatrists who had recently joined the practice. Joanna Watson, the psychologist who left the phone message, was his very first addition to the growing psychiatric practice that he and Elsa had established in Chesterfield, a wealthy suburb of Saint Louis. *Oh well,* he thought. *I guess I don't really have anything planned for the day. I might as well stop by and see how things are going.*

Joel's former Chesterfield office was located in a newly built office complex in the Chesterfield Valley in West Saint Louis County. After the Missouri River flooded the entire Chesterfield Valley during the flood of '93, most of the businesses located there were razed, the levees were reinforced, and the City gave permission for new development to begin. Within ten years, the valley was fully developed, complete with four and five story medical office buildings, chain and specialty restaurants, and strip malls stretching end to end across the entire length of the valley. The lobby of Joel's former office had a centrally located fountain at the entrance of the building. All floors were tiled in expensive granite. Lush, tropical greenery lined the monstrous windows, granting the plants seemingly unlimited access to the enormous amounts of Missouri sunshine beaming down on the building's southern face.

Joel's former office was located on the third floor. As he entered, he encountered the familiar face of Ariel, seated at the reception desk. Although she acknowledged his presence immediately, Joel noticed that she was setting an appointment with a patient on the phone. He had also noticed that the traditional handset phones had been replaced by a headset, which Ariel had now wrapped around her head. She spoke politely into the microphone wrapped around her chin, smiling at Joel while she spoke.

"So, Doctor Ormond will see you at 11 A.M. on Friday, the twelfth. Please be sure to bring your insurance card at the time of your visit. See you then." She pressed the button to hang up the call, removed her headset, got up, and almost skipped over to greet Joel. She gave him a big hug.

"Well, look who the cat dragged in!"

Joel responded, smiling also. "Well, how the heck are you, little girl?" He pulled back and looked into her face. He picked up a small lock of her, now shoulder length, hair between his thumb and forefinger. "No more pink?"

"No," she looked down, shyly. "You know, I'll be twenty-nine next June. I'm back to my natural color. And I'm kinda growing it out."

"Maybe Joanna has gotten to you after all these years, huh? What are you doing with yourself these days?"

"Got a new boyfriend. He's a drummer in our band. You know, we're really doing well these days. We're starting to get more gigs out of town, and we just released our second CD."

"Anything I've heard?"

"Probably not. We get some local airplay, but not a lot just yet. We have practice space at the old Lemp Brewery. I'll give you a tour sometime."

"Sounds like fun. I love new musical experiences. Will I need to turn down my hearing aid?"

"Oh, stop...." She fake slapped his arm. "You're pretty cool for an old guy." At that moment, Joanna came out of her office and made her way over to Joel and Ariel. Ariel whispered as an aside to Joel, not moving her lips. "You're not nearly as stuffy as some other people around here." She hinted to Joanna, who moved toward them.

Joanna looked at Joel, "So you got my message? Have a moment?"

Joel nodded and followed her to her office. On his way, he passed the door to his old office, noticing a new name plate on the door—*Dr. Michael Ormond, M.D.* There was a young man, standing behind Joel's old mahogany desk, unpacking a box. *There's the younger model*, Joel thought to himself. He walked on.

The two made their way into Joanna's office. Everything was, as he remembered, meticulously set in place. Her Stanford diploma, along with her licenses and graduation photo, were leveled and carefully spaced on her back office wall in coordinated document frames. She had some more feminine objets d'art dotting the credenza and the end table next to the couch by the window. But all in all, it was a fairly unobtrusive décor. Joanna had taken great pains to make her office appear that way for the benefit of her patients—a neutral environment in which to confide their intimate secrets.

Joanna motioned for Joel to be seated before her desk. As she sat also, Joel peered out Joanna's open office door down the hallway toward Ariel, also seated behind the reception counter. Joanna excused herself for a moment to check on some voice mail messages and picked up her phone. Joel sat patiently, watching Ariel, recalling how different she had become from the girl Elsa had initially hired ten years before.

After years of working downtown in Barnes-Jewish Hospital's psychiatric ward, Joel's wife, Elsa, convinced him to open a private practice in 1998 in West Saint Louis County. In addition, he took on a position in the behavioral health wing at St. John's Mercy Medical Center Hospital in Creve Coeur. He made patient rounds in the morning and saw his private patients at his new office in the afternoons. In the beginning, Elsa managed the patient load at the private practice, acting as office manager. But after two years, his practice had blossomed to the point where Elsa was soon overwhelmed by the tasks of setting appointments, and handling and filing countless insurance forms and patient records.

He remembered meeting Ariel for the first time. Elsa sat behind the reception desk, attempting to handle multiple appointments simultaneously, buried behind mountains of patient files. Joel stood behind her, trying to find one particular file, with no luck. Ariel had just turned nineteen. She had short, bright, bubble-gum pink hair spiked into an asymmetric, Victoria Beckham-ish bob. She dressed entirely in black. A snug black sweater and short skirt accentuated her curvy, petite frame. She had intense, huge, dark-brown eyes, thickly lined with black eyeliner, and almost doll-like lips, which were exaggerated by deep red lipstick. She also sported a long black overcoat, black fish net stockings, and black stiletto boots. She had a few visible tattoos (Joel only assumed that there were plenty of other tattoos obscured beneath her dark outfit), and several piercings, which included a dainty diamond in her nose, two holes and rings in her right ear, and a series of holes and silver earrings lining the entire outer edge of her left ear.

"I hear you're looking for some part-time office help," Ariel stated.

Joel and Elsa looked out beyond the mountain of files. Even though Dr. Russell had encountered some unique individuals during the course of his practice, he sat speechless. Elsa, on the other hand, never lost her composure, even in the strangest of company. If she was shocked by Ariel's appearance in the least, she failed to show it.

"Well," Elsa responded, "We were looking for someone with a little experience to help out in front here." She answered.

"I used to work for Doctor Goldstein two floors down," Ariel replied.

"I see. Why did you leave?" Joel asked.

"Well," Ariel hesitated. "He fired me."

"Is that so?" Elsa inquired calmly. "Why is that?"

"He said that I wore too much black, and it depressed his patients."

Elsa appreciated her candor and snickered. "Well, I surmise that Doctor Goldstein's patients were probably depressed because they had to see Doctor Goldstein. I think he's a bit of a stuffed shirt myself. Well, just exactly what is it that you can do?" Elsa asked.

Ariel pointed to the mountains of files at the edge of the reception desk. "For starters, I can help you file that!" she stated confidently.

Without even looking back to consult with Joel, Elsa asked, "Can you start now?"

Ariel immediately set her belongings down and went to work.

Now, Joel noted, Ariel had softened in appearance. Her hair had grown, and she was back to her normal shade of a dark, ash brown. Today, she wore a more muted color of a celadon green dress, with coordinating heels. Her flattering figure had not changed, but she seemed now less intent on making a social statement and more concerned with looking professional. He was grateful to hear, however, that she had not given up her dream of being a successful singer. He sometimes remembered hearing her sing softly to herself in the office, when she thought no one could hear. Her voice sounded sweet and pleasant.

Chapter 2- Late to the Office

Joel sat patiently in Joanna's office, waiting for her to check her messages. Then Joanna hung up the phone. "I'm sorry about that, Joel." She suddenly turned serious. "Listen, Joel. I know you noticed that Doctor Ormond has taken over your office."

Joel didn't respond.

She tried to explain. "I didn't know what else to do. I was floundering over here. We have a successful practice, and we couldn't keep up anymore. You refused to see patients, and we found Mike to handle new patients and the few patients you had left here."

She rose and moved toward a box of Joel's belongings on the back corner floor of her office. She picked up the box and placed it in the chair next to Joel. "I'm sorry, Joel. I know you loved Elsa, but it's like you've been suspended in time for the last—how long?"

"Seven years," Joel responded.

"—seven years, and you don't seem to want help. I know you feel bad about her death, and I'm sorry. You need closure, and I'm not sure, in your present state, that you will ever find what you're looking for. But, in the meantime, you have left me in charge of this thriving practice, and the rest of us living here have got to figure out how to pay the bills. Mike isn't you, but he's stable and dependable. That's what we need right now." Joanna paused, looking apologetic. She moved back, sitting on the front edge of her desk.

Joel still didn't respond.

After an additional pause and realizing that Joel was probably not going to answer, Joanna continued, "That's not all, Joel. I got a call from Sam Fredrickson about Jake Sternen. It seems he escaped from the hospital two days ago, and they wanted me to warn you."

Joel remained motionless. "Escaped?"

"Yes," Joanna answered. "I know what you're thinking, Joel. But when he realized what he had done, he was very remorseful. He never intended to hurt anyone but you. And—you treated him, Joel, you know—he was a diagnosed Paranoid Schizophrenic *with* PTSD. After he understood the consequences of his actions and how he had killed an innocent woman, it took the winds out of his delusional sail, so to speak."

She looked at Joel's face which was, at this point, expressionless. His silence seemed to make her even more uneasy, so she continued her explanation. "Joel, they don't think he's a threat at this point. He's been compliant with his meds since his sentencing. And Sam tells me it is not likely that they will even publicize the fact that he is missing. The Army would like to keep this all under wraps, because they don't think it would help the war effort in Afghanistan if word got out that a crazed and murderous ex-Army Sergeant was on the loose."

"Do they have any idea where he might have gone?"

"I'm not sure he has any living family connections here at all. That would mean there would be no reason for him to stick around here." She tried to assuage Joel's apparent doubts. "Really, Joel... I don't think he has any interest in you at all..."

"I'm sure he doesn't," Joel agreed. "He probably wants to move on like the rest of the world. Everyone except me, that is."

Joanna moved forward and put her hand on his shoulder. For a brief second, Joel remembered a time when she had been willing to touch much more than that. But at this point in his life, and looking the way he did, an assuring touch on the shoulder was as good a relationship with a woman as he would probably ever get again. He couldn't believe that he once secured the heart of this attractive and intelligent woman. He couldn't comprehend how a woman like Joanna would ever look up to him as a mentor or confidant or even have ever desired him as a man.

Joel took his box of belongings, which consisted of his Washington University and Yale diplomas, psychiatric books and papers he had published throughout the years, old photos of him and Elsa, an old paperweight he had proudly blown by hand in an undergraduate art class, and files and session tapes he had made during consultations with former patients. Included also in the box was the old tape recorder he used to tape his sessions—a mini tape recorder, probably still functional, but now outdated in today's digital age. It seemed that everything he had ever accomplished during his lifetime had now been reduced to a simple box of stuff, now largely useless junk.

On the way home, Joel thought more about Joanna. He remembered making the initial decision to hire her. He decided that he needed another associate to offer therapy to his growing number of Chesterfield housewives, who attempted to make better sense of their privileged but seemingly directionless lives. He was barely able to meet the demands of prescribing antidepressants and Xanax for this depressed, substance-addicted, and anxiety-ridden group. Both he and Elsa agreed that he needed someone prepared to listen to the endless drivel about dance camp, book clubs, cheating husbands, SUVs, and thieving housemaids.

Joel had actually made the decision to hire Joanna in 2001, based on her exemplary credentials and a phone interview he conducted with her while she still lived in California. When she actually appeared before him in the office for the first time, he was pleased to see how truly attractive she was. Like Elsa, when he first met her, Joanna was beautiful. She dressed simply, yet she still looked sophisticated and professional. She had auburn hair, ice blue eyes, and had applied makeup meticulously but sparingly, as if to say, "Here, I have taken care to make myself look better, but really, I wake up in the morning looking this beautiful." Although she was young, she possessed an air of self-confidence, much like the air of self-confidence that Elsa exuded when he first met her.

Joanna pretty much had the job at Joel's practice before she entered the office for the first time. This decision had already been made by him. When she came to see Joel after she had moved to Chesterfield from California, she dressed in a tan, well-tailored skirt suit. She was also wore pearl earrings—no doubt real pearls. Strands of her auburn hair were pulled back loosely, while the rest of her wavy locks cascaded down her shoulders.

Elsa and Ariel were filing together when Joanna walked in. "Hello," She greeted. "I'm here to see Doctor Joel Russell. I'm Joanna Watson." Unlike the many pharmaceutical reps, who paraded through the office and made at least a hollow effort to get to know the office staff, Joanna made no attempt to get to know Elsa or Ariel. She did not ask their names.

Seeming offended, Elsa walked to Joel's open door, speaking loud enough for Joanna to hear. Addressing Joel, she called to him, "Your majesty, Doctor Joanna Watson, Ph.D. is here to meet you!" Joel walked out to greet Joanna and invite her into his office. This was their first face-to-face encounter, and Joel was satisfied to discover that Joanna's appearance was actually even more pleasant than her telephone voice.

Joanna was twenty-five, gorgeous, and very young. Although love and the complexities of sexual relationships were something she studied and knew well in textbooks and in clinic, she had not known much of a serious relationship herself. She had one or two steady boyfriends in college, but she found herself often becoming bored with trying to satisfy the desires and superficial needs of men her own age. She was much more intelligent and mature than they were. *She needs someone much older*, Joel often thought.

Being committed to Elsa and having to fulfill his duties on staff at St. Johns as well as keeping up with his private practice gave Joel very little time to think about Joanna in anything but a professional way. At times, he would be momentarily distracted by her long, curvy legs or her pouty lips. But this distraction was only short-lived. He soon refocused on the task at hand. For the most part, they did not even work together much, since his job at the practice was primarily to regulate medication, and hers was to provide therapy.

Rarely, Joanna would confide in Joel about her dissatisfaction with having to treat the issues of some of her clients. Often, she would state how unfulfilled she was by the fact that she had worked so hard at university to be able to ultimately help people in need. Yet here she was, wasting her life treating mainly women with no *real* problems to speak of.

Her patients were primarily housewives of Chesterfield who came to therapy, because it afforded them an opportunity to pay a "professional" once a week to listen for fifty straight minutes while they droned on about their boring lives. They were often housewives of prominent and successful businessmen, wealthy enough to employ their own staff of domestic employees. Several of the luckier ones employed nannies for the few children they had, and the rest tried to occupy their days with combinations of Pilates sessions, shopping, fine dining, hosting an occasional dinner party, volunteering their time to local charitable organizations, and attending a weekly therapy session with Joanna. They often drank too much white wine, and they relied on Joel to prescribe them the antidepressants and benzodiazepines which helped them deal with the anxiety of their suburban housewife lives. Joanna once stated that her typical client was as "obtuse as that door there," (pointing to her sturdy and very dense office door). Often, if Joel would catch a glimpse of her escorting a patient out after session, she would make eye contact with him and roll her eyes. How she longed for a patient with *real* problems.

About a year after Joanna began seeing patients at the practice, Joel had learned that a mutual patient of his and Joanna's had killed herself. She had taken an overdose of Desyrel, an antidepressant, along with a cocktail of several common antipsychotic and benzodiazepine drugs she had hoarded over the course of the year. Although this was not Joel's first patient lost to suicide, it was Joanna's. When she heard the news about her patient's death, Joanna became distraught and shaken. Joel had called her into his office to break the news to her, where she broke out into near hysterics, confessing to Joel that she felt she was to blame for neglecting the needs of the recently deceased patient.

Joel tried to console her by telling her she was not at fault. He assured Joanna that he knew she tried to help, but sometimes, "....you do lose a patient. You can't save every patient who comes to you for help," he assured. "You can only hope to help most of them and learn from any mistakes you may have made with the others."

"No, Joel. You don't understand," she cried. "It *is* my fault she died. See, this patient would constantly threaten to kill herself. I had her hospitalized several times over the last couple of years. Then, it became tedious. I felt she was trying to hollowly threaten me to get me to spend more time with her. First, I did everything I was supposed to do. I began to make contracts and to schedule more frequent sessions with her during the week. When that wasn't enough, she would call the exchange in the middle of the night. I would encourage her to admit herself to the ER, and once I even called the police! There were several times when I tried to get her to check in to the hospital, but she would refuse to admit herself.

"One night, she called the exchange at 3 A.M. and stated that she planned to kill herself if I didn't call her back in ten minutes. When I called her, she wasn't at all suicidal. As a matter of fact, she had been driving herself crazy ruminating about some stupid seating arrangement for her daughter's upcoming wedding. I lost it. I told her that she had abused our doctor/client relationship, and that she had destroyed my trust in her by continuously crying 'wolf' when she had no intention of killing herself. I felt she was manipulating me for attention, and I told her that we would talk about it at our next session. I was just frustrated and tired. I had no idea......" Joanna sobbed.

"Look, Joanna, I know you feel responsible for this. But even though this *is* our job, we *are* human, and we *do* make mistakes. We are *not* responsible for the happiness or the bad choices others make—even those who are entrusted into our care."

Joanna continued sobbing, glancing up at her mentor through a veil of tears.

"You are a beautiful, caring human being. You did the best you could. You can't go through life believing that you are the cause of this woman's death. You tried to help."

Joanna's sobbing continued, and it became clear to Joel that her hysterics were less about her patient and more about herself. "You don't understand! I have *nobody*, Joel! All I have is this. I've worked so hard during my lifetime, and I am a slave to these women who, in large part, I resent and sometimes even hate! You and Elsa—you are so blessed. You have each other. I'm just going to rot here, wasting my days listening to bored housewives blather on about their meaningless existences. I have nobody who cares about me or needs me or loves me. What's wrong with me, Joel?"

Joel stared at Joanna in disbelief. "There is nothing wrong with you. You are perfect. Look at you, Joanna. You're so bright, and you're absolutely gorgeous. You have a prosperous career, and you have an entire lifetime ahead of you. And—look at me, Joanna—you have *me*. *I* care about you...."

Right at that moment, Joel realized his true feelings for Joanna. He suddenly understood how desperately he needed to be close to her. He never before allowed himself the luxury of experiencing feelings for her. But having Joanna there in front of him, vulnerable to him, with the opportunity now present, he understood that Joanna had also harbored mutual feelings of attraction for him. He no longer worried where or how her feelings for him were rooted. He no longer cared whether these feelings were wrong or right. He felt a burning need to kiss her. He wanted to be close to her, and he wanted her in his life. He didn't care that her feelings might be misplaced feelings for him as a mentor or a father figure. He wanted to kiss her, and he knew she wanted it.

Joel leaned forward to wipe Joanna's tear, and finally gave in to his urge to kiss her. Her lips felt warm, soft, and inviting to him. She responded by reaching out to him, grasping his arm and pulling him toward her. He sensed her soft and sweet tongue pressed between his lips. He felt her searching, and he felt his heart pounding harder than he had felt it pound in many years. He moved to loosen her long auburn hair by unfastening her hair clip. He leaned back to watch her hair, now loose, fall innocently about her shoulders.

Joel kissed Joanna again, only this time, the kiss grew fiercer and more passionate. His heart beat stronger, as did hers. As he moved his left hand to cup her soft, heaving breast from beneath her silk blouse, he could even feel how passionately her heart was beating. His breath grew short, as she fumbled to unbutton his crisp cotton shirt. He pulled at his necktie desperately, and before he knew it, most of his attire had been cast to the floor. She was still partially clothed, but her brassiere was unfastened, and her breasts were now exposed. She leaned back, still seated on the patient chair in front of Joel's great mahogany desk. Her pink nipples were erect, and he kneeled before her.

Joel reached under Joanna's skirt and felt his way to her dainty lace panties. Reaching with the other hand, he pulled them down past her supple thighs down her long legs. He tossed them over his shoulder into the growing heap of shed clothing. As he tossed the panties, without looking, he tried to look ludicrously suave, and Joanna giggled.

He stopped for a moment to savor what now lay exposed beneath her skirt. As he delicately touched her moist clitoris with his forefinger, she closed her eyes and leaned back. Soon, she was writhing in ecstasy and on the verge of climax.

He could bear it no longer. He didn't wait for permission. He wanted to lead. He was in control. He entered her, because he now realized how close he needed to be to her. He took her, not only as if it were their first time together, but as if it was something that they would never share again. They were governed by their desires, and they were connecting in a way they had always desired to, but never realized until this moment. For the first time, he was not being judged, only desired by a beautiful woman as a desirable man.

Although Elsa was the furthest thing from his mind at that moment and during the year Joel carried on this affair, he felt that his relationship with Joanna was very different from what he and Elsa had. Elsa was far from vulnerable. She seldom lost her composure in even the most devastating and precarious of situations. Elsa's feelings for Joel were that of mutual attraction—a love of equals—at times romantic, at times companionate. Joanna was young and full of life. Joanna looked up to him. And, for the first time in any romantic relationship, Joel was the one who called the shots. Joel was the one in charge. And Joanna was perfectly fine with that.

From then, the moment of their first kiss, and up until the time of Elsa's death, Joel and Joanna carried on their affair, looking for every opportunity to pursue their forbidden relationship. Their encounters would be spontaneous, but sometimes there might be a meticulously planned rendezvous at a hotel or Joanna's apartment. Because they shared the same office, each knew the other's appointment roster. Rarely, their liaisons occurred right there in a deserted office after hours—in his office or hers. Once, Joel recalled, smirking devilishly, he tried plowing her, half-naked, in a fit of passion right on the receptionist's counter, when they were almost discovered by the housekeeping staff.

Joel chose the field of psychiatry because he understood his personality was unlike most of the men he considered friends and associates. Of course, he was a normal male with normal male desires. Growing up, he experienced the standard male experiences regarding his growing attraction to females and coming to grips with his male sexuality. But, unlike his other male counterparts, he was somewhat of a loner. He never had an interest in watching weekend football with the guys. Although he joined a fraternity, he justified his membership by stating that it was an academic fraternity and not a social one. He often found himself hanging with female friends, most of them platonic, who felt they could open up to him, because he understood and was a good listener. It was not that he wasn't interested in having a physical relationship with these women. It was just that they almost always considered him as nothing more than a friend.

Joanna truly desired him. And he desired her. But Joanna seemed to perceive Joel differently than other women did, including Elsa. Joanna saw him as powerful, masculine, desirable, and spontaneous.

And Joel enjoyed the idea that he could be uninhibited with her. She saw him as strong and powerful. He perceived her to be feminine and vulnerable. They both perceived each other to be, in the bedroom, someone quite the opposite of their public office persona. Perhaps that was the reason they finally chose to have the affair. Joel and Joanna enabled each other to live out their most intimate personal fantasies by seeing each other as someone very different from who they really were.

After thinking about his former affair with Joanna, and after recalling how she worshiped Joel in the beginning, he became sad to think about how she might perceive him now. Did she think he was a mistake she wished she could forget? Even worse, did she perceive him as a horny, pathetic, old man, who deserved nothing but pity? She was still so gorgeous—a little older and wiser, perhaps, but still quite captivating. He didn't know her anymore, and he wondered how things might have been if they had decided to spend the rest of their lives together.

Despite their many indiscretions and near-misses, Elsa never suspected a thing about Joel's infidelity—that is, until the very end. But Joel was tired of thinking, and he didn't want to think about that now.

Chapter 3- Packing up Memories

Ellen Rodriguez was a neighbor and real estate agent, who had the unfortunate habit of often dropping by on neighbors unannounced. She was so bold that she was one of the few individuals in the neighborhood who still had the testicles to drop by Joel's to check in on him. She was not a particularly caring individual—more nosey than anything else.

Ellen was a divorcée, who lived just down the road from Joel. She had been divorced for over ten years, and her two boys were now both in college. Her cardiologist ex-husband's alimony checks still supported most of her flamboyant lifestyle of countless shopping sprees to the Galleria and Plaza Frontenac malls. But she decided to start selling real estate shortly after her divorce to keep her busy with something other than having to be a single mother. She enjoyed adult conversation and interests and didn't really relate well to children.

She had long, blonde hair, which she always wore down about her shoulders, believing that hairstyle made her look more youthful. Today she wore stilettos and a very short skirt, which showed off her toned thighs and legs. She had luscious, large lips, which she used to blow kisses to friends and colleagues when she bid them goodbye. Joel thought that perhaps she fancied herself a sort of modern day Marilyn Monroe.

"You know, Joel, you should really consider selling this place. I mean, you don't even use most of the rooms in this house. It's obviously way too big for you. Granted, you would have to move your stuff out. There is a lot of clutter, here—and dust." She snobbily wiped dust from the coffee table and clapped her hands together. "I could bring my man, Stan, out here to bring back that beautiful rose garden Lillian had nurtured to give this place a little curb appeal. You could fetch 2.5 million easily in a pinch."

Joel shrugged.

"Think about it. And you can get those nasty city officials off your back about how you let this place go. Really, Joel. Think about it."

Joel did think about it. He seemed to do a lot of thinking lately. It almost seemed as if his mind had been empty for the last seven years—like he had lived in an emotional limbo. Everything he touched, everybody whom he met lately, everything that had happened to him recently, seemed to trigger long repressed memories he had tried so hard to forget.

After several days of introspection, Joel decided that it would be best to sell Elsa's family estate. She had no successors or distant family heir who had an interest in the property, and this home had only served to perpetuate memories and feelings which Joel felt would be better to let go. If he purged his life of this chapter, maybe he could forget all the terrible mistakes of his past and heal from the loss of his beloved Elsa. *Yes,* he thought. *Selling the house might be the answer. Perhaps I can get closure and move forward with my life.*

This time, Joel approached Ellen. "I have decided to sell Elsa's family estate." He was Elsa's only living family and the sole heir of her estate, but he never really regarded it as *his* home. He was never made to feel ill at ease at her mother's home. On the contrary—he was always treated as an honored guest. Even though he had stayed at the estate for almost thirty years, he had never worn out his welcome.

Ellen placed her realty sign out in Joel's front yard even before he could finish signing the contract authorizing her to put the house on the market. Immediately, she listed the tasks he would be required to perform to get the home in order. She pointed to his stack of medical and Houdini books scattered about the living room. "We need to put all this stuff in storage. Joel, I need you to help me get this house showplace ready."

Joel agreed, and he did acknowledge that he had accumulated a sizeable number of possessions over the years. *It is time to purge my life of all its unnecessary complications,* he thought. *I need to start fresh.*

For the first time in a long time, Joel pushed his way through the Visqueen curtains blocking his entrance to the rest of the uninhabited portion of the estate. This included the dining room, den, several storage rooms on the first floor, and five bedrooms and two full baths located upstairs. Ellen had provided him with brand new moving boxes, complete with strapping tape, styrofoam peanuts, and bubble wrap for breakables.

First, he started packing the contents of the massive china cabinet and buffet in the dining room. He carefully fingered a delicate tea cup, pulled from the china cabinet and made of fine, bone Noritake china. He recalled the day he and Elsa chose to register for their wedding china, and how they arrived at that selected pattern. Actually, Joel was the one who chose the pattern. Knowing he would be living at Elsa's home, he felt that pattern would be best suited to the motif of the house.

Joel carefully removed each cup, saucer, plate, and bowl from the cabinet, wrapping every item in bubble wrap. *This is the care I should afford each selected item in this home*, he thought. He should treat each item which Elsa had once touched as if he were touching Elsa. He should confront the task as if Elsa were present, supervising the whole affair.

Soon, however, Joel felt overwhelmed with the task he had postponed for so many years, when he realized how monumental the task truly was. *There is just a lot of shit in this place*, he thought. And he did not have the time or the stamina to do this all this carefully with all this crap. He thought of the latest episode he had seen of the show *Hoarders*. Then, he thought of the many homeless individuals he had treated in the psychiatric hospital over the course of the last thirty years. He thought about how these often mentally ill individuals were unable to maintain any normalcy in their daily existence, having no home to return to at the end of the day. They hauled all their prized belongings with them in trash bags, pushed them in stolen shopping carts, and transported them along by other, more creative means. Your home was where you kept your stuff. The more stuff you carried with you, the sweeter your home was, and the more secure you felt about the nature of your existence. *I think I might like to be a hobo someday*, Joel thought. He snickered to himself and decided he liked the word "hobo", despite the fact that it had long been politically incorrect.

Joel moved to Elsa's office. He sat at her antique, Rococo-style desk, placed his hand on the first framed portrait sitting there, and paused before attempting to pack it into a smaller box. He exercised less care packing now, but he paused more and more to consider all the items that he stored away.

The first picture was of Elsa as a young girl, before they met. In the picture, Elsa was smiling. Perhaps she was seventeen. But she looked much the same as she did the day they first met. She must have been twenty-two at that time.

It was 1981. Elsa had just graduated from college. Joel was twenty-six. He had just begun his residency at Washington University, and both he and his colleagues were attending a gala for Barnes Hospital's new psychiatric facility, which had just opened in downtown St. Louis.

Joel chose to play the wallflower that evening. His purpose was simply to make an appearance, and he did not feel compelled to network or hobnob in an effort to further his career. He seemed perfectly content to stand next to the bar, nursing his beer.

That is when he noticed Elsa across the room. She was absolutely gorgeous, poised, and demure. She was working the crowd, greeting each physician, administrator, and patron by name—as if she knew them all her life. She was a petite woman. Her medium length, chestnut hair was simply coifed into an elegant French twist. Her full lips conveyed an unusually warm and inviting smile, which was delicately framed by her perfect nose and naturally rosy, high cheekbones. She wore a minimal amount of jewelry—two carat diamond posts in each ear. Her beautiful, hazel eyes were enhanced with very little makeup, and she wore an elegant, tea-length, royal blue beaded gown. Joel knew it was tailored by some sleek designer, but he never paid attention to that. What impressed him about Elsa was that she appeared to move from patron to patron gracefully, never missing a beat. It was almost as if she flitted around the great hall like a rare butterfly.

A skilled, five-piece jazz band played old stand-ards for the crowd. At the center of the great ballroom was a spacious hardwood dance floor, but no one was dancing. The socialites and physicians' wives were content to mill around, and the administrators were happy simply raising donations for the recently completed project from any potential latecomers who might think to contribute. Joel and his other wallflower colleagues stood apart and simply talked shop. *It's a shame no one is dancing,* Joel thought. *But then again, these are scientists, and scientists are not usually noted for their dancing skills.*

Joel, however, was a skilled ballroom dancer. He actually studied theatre for a time at Yale and danced with both grace and flexibility. In addition, he could sing, act, and played cocktail piano quite well. His creativity, he felt, helped make him as intuitive as he was scientific, which is why he thought he would make a good psychiatrist. None of his colleagues knew of these talents, which he had neglected in recent years. Some would probably have guessed that Joel did not enjoy the limelight, since he seemed to shy away from the public eye. But that night, seeing Elsa across the room, he felt empowered to show her his more cultured side.

Elsa had noticed Joel standing on the sidelines. She would glance at Joel occasionally from across the room, while engaged in conversation. At that time, she stood before a dermatologist, who seemed to be talking incessantly about himself. She listened politely, half-heartedly interested in what he had to say. Occasionally, the dermatologist would make grand gestures with his arms, and Elsa would nod, smile, and glance over at Joel. Joel put down his beer, and walked across the room to approach Elsa.

"Excuse me, Miss. I don't know if you have noticed, but someone has hired this marvelous jazz band to play for this affair, and not one couple is dancing. Would you care to dance with me?" Joel stretched out his arm to lead her onto the dance floor.

"Yes. I would like that." Elsa replied. She excused herself and followed Joel to the center of the deserted floor. He reached his right arm around the back of her small waist, and held her right hand in his left. He hadn't danced with a woman in five years, but he was still quite agile.

"Why, sir. You are a skilled dancer. Imagine that." She glanced down at his name tag. "—and very handsome, I might add. What kind of medicine do you practice, Doctor Joel Russell, M.D.?"

"I am a psychiatrist—a resident here at the university hospital," he answered.

"And you? What is it that you do, Miss—"

"Elsa. My name is Elsa. Well, I don't do much of anything. I am an heiress."

"An heiress?"

"Why, yes." They stop dancing for a moment. She turned to point to an older woman at the front of the room, whom Elsa clearly resembled and who stood, conversing with several other doctors. "See that woman? She is my mother. She is worth millions.

And when she kicks off, *I* will be worth millions." Elsa smiled as she then pointed to herself.

They continued dancing. "Does that make me more attractive to you, Doctor Joel Russell, M.D.?" She exaggerated his name dramatically and humorously.

Joel smiled. "Well, Miss Elsa, I'm not sure any amount of money could make you more beautiful than you are to me at this moment."

Elsa smiled. "You, sir, are quite the charmer..."

"But having lots of money doesn't hurt."

Elsa and Joel both laughed.

Once Joel and Elsa began dancing, several other couples tried to join them on the dance floor. The party had warmed up and was soon in full gear. Joel and Elsa spent most of the evening together, dancing and talking about their lives, their duties, and their dreams and aspirations. Joel had decided that during his short life of twenty-six years, and during his clinical training, he had never met an individual so uniquely compelling as Elsa. She was brilliant, fun, and—most of all—the most beautiful woman he had ever met. Although he would normally be intimidated by her wealth, he didn't care that she had money. He cared that she took a shine to him. The entire evening she made him feel empowered, important, and engaging. He felt that way, because Elsa made him feel that way. She made *everyone* feel special.

At the end of the evening, Joel walked Elsa out to valet parking. He held her hand and kissed her cheek goodnight. "Goodnight, Doctor Joel Russell, M.D.," she said. "I hope we will be seeing each other again."

Chapter 4- Remembering Lillian

Joel packed Elsa's graduation photo in the box. The next photo to be placed in the box was that of Elsa's mother, Lillian, posing with Elsa and Elsa's father, who had died before Joel met her. Elsa was maybe seven years old. Lillian had a "Jackie Kennedy" look about her. Her expression was a sterner one than Elsa's, but Joel knew that her sternness was a façade. Elsa soon learned how to break through Lillian's austerity to expose her marshmallow interior. And, once Lillian realized that Joel and Elsa were truly in love, Lillian treated Joel like a son.

He recalled his first meeting with Lillian.

Joel approached the vast Tudor-style manor, having just parked his tattered Datsun in the center of the large, circular drive at its entrance. He brushed off the lapel of his heavy, tweed jacket and then lifted and slammed the heavy iron door knocker several times. Expecting a servant to answer, Joel was surprised that Elsa answered.

"You look shocked to see me answer the door," she mocked. "The butler is off-duty today." She ushered Joel in. "No, actually, I'm kidding. We don't even *have* a butler. This house is powered by estrogen."

She turned to her mother, who suddenly appeared in the doorway—a stately woman, dressed in a lavender tunic and a coordinating floral skirt. She wore several strands of opera-length beads around her neck. Her hair was white, but it was beautifully coifed in an elegant but feminine short style. Joel knew that Elsa had inherited all her good looks from Lillian, along with Lillian's impeccable sense of style. Her face seemed like an older version of her daughter's. True, her face sported a few wrinkles, but her high cheekbones and remarkably warm smile were almost identical to Elsa's. She possessed a larger frame than her daughter's more petite frame, but she was by no means overweight.

"Mother, I would like to introduce you to Doctor Joel Russell. Joel, this is Mother."

Lillian took Joel's hand firmly. "Please call me Lillian. It is a pleasure to make your acquaintance." Lillian smiled. "My daughter has talked a great deal about you. She really seems to be quite smitten with you."

Joel laughed softly.

"Yes, I do date myself. I suppose 'smitten' is a term not often used these days, is it?" Lillian asked this question rhetorically. She was quite aware of her anti-quated vocabulary.

"'In lust' seems more 1980s, Mother." Elsa winked, then smiled at Joel.

Embarrassed, Joel began to stutter. "I..I find your daughter exceptionally beautiful and charming, myself. I suppose you could say I'm smitten with her." He winked back at Elsa.

"Shall we be seated? Dinner is ready." Lillian motioned Joel to be seated at the dinner table.

The family dinner table was surprisingly modest, compared to the massive chandelier suspended above. It could comfortably seat eight but wasn't so enormous that three diners could not easily pass serving bowls to one another. Joel sat across the table from Elsa, who was clearly flirting with him. Lillian attempted to engage him in pleasant conversation.

"So Joel, exactly what are you a doctor of?" Lillian inquired.

"Psychiatry. I have just started my residency at Wash U."

"Is that so? Well, that's a plus. I believe some of our family ancestors could probably have used a little psychiatric assistance. What caused you to decide on that specialty?"

As Joel took a moment to fashion an intelligent response, he became aware of the fact that Elsa had absolutely no interest in the conversation at hand. Instead, she seemed intent on distracting him. As she smiled devilishly at him, she quietly kicked off her right heel beneath the table and erotically swept the calf beneath his trousered pant leg.

Immediately startled, Joel stuttered again, trying to act cool. "I suppose....I find the human mind more fascinating than the body......Plus, I fainted twice in first year gross anatomy lab."

Lillian chuckled only once. "I'm sure you're being modest, Doctor Russell. I know for a fact that my daughter wouldn't be so taken with you, unless you were as gifted as you are obviously charming." Without missing a beat, Lillian turned to Elsa, "Dear, stop playing footsie with the boy and pass the soup!"

Chapter 5- The Wedding Photo and The Piano

Joel had almost completely cleared Elsa's desk of memories and stored them into the box, with the exception of the last framed photo of their wedding. He brushed the dust from the frame and ran his hand over the twenty-eight year old photograph. Then he carefully placed the photo in the box and opened the desk drawer to find a yellowed copy of their wedding invitation. He read the date of the ceremony—May 23, 1982. Unsuccessfully, he tried to read it aloud, but it was almost as if he regarded that date, like Elsa's name, as if it were something so sacred, it shouldn't be uttered matter-of-factly. He closed his eyes and vividly recalled their wedding day.

The Japanese irises of the Missouri Botanical Gardens bloomed slightly later than the traditional American variety. And, since Joel and Elsa chose to marry in late May, the flowers were—everything was—perfect that day. Since neither bride nor groom had any serious religious affiliation at this point in their lives, they chose instead a neutral, yet terrifically beautiful scene in which to recite their vows. But, to appease the few elite guests of Saint Louis society, a prominent and willing minister was asked to preside over the affair.

After the ceremony, they held a reception in and around the nearby Linnaean House, located near the entrance to the Botanical Gardens. About 250 guests were in attendance, most of them members of Saint Louis's elite—prominent physicians, judges, professors, artists, celebrities, and even a few sports figures—all familiar family acquaintances and/or business partners. Joel, Elsa, and Elsa's mother, along with the small party of bridesmaids and groomsmen, lined up at the front of the reception hall to greet incoming guests.

Robert Gaynor, a young Saint Louis alderman and prominent lawyer slightly older than Joel, greeted Elsa with a kiss on the cheek. "How are you darling? You are simply radiant today!"

Elsa smiled and introduced the family friend to Joel, who acknowledged Robert and shook his hand.

"Tell me, old boy......What is your secret?"

"I'm sorry?" Joel asked. He looked a bit per-plexed.

"Yes. Your secret. I've known Elsa for years and had a crush on her. How did a regular guy like you manage to snatch up one of Saint Louis's most eligible bachelorettes?"

Joel only responded with a nod and a smile. He didn't need any man to remind him of how lucky he was. He knew he was the luckiest man alive.

Joel made his way into the music room. Initially, the room was considered a den, but Lillian turned the room into a conservatory when she learned that Joel was an accomplished pianist. He was classically trained, but he chose to play by ear, improvising jazz tunes and cocktail piano pieces he had heard instead of practicing Bach, Beethoven, and Chopin, as his piano instructor had insisted. As a result, he was a horrible sight reader, and, he surmised, the source of recurrent nightmares for his old German piano teacher, if she were still alive.

He recalled many occasions, when he came to a lesson after having been assigned a new piece the previous week. Often, he would open the music, seeing it for the very first time. He would plod through about twelve measures of sheer hell, all the while hearing his instructor's sighs of disgust. Eventually, she would beg him to stop, and ask, "Did you practice at all last week?"

Ashamed, Joel would always shake his head, "No." But, when it came time to practice, he would simply play whatever pleased him. He had a great ear, and upon hearing a song on the radio after just a short time, could pick out whatever tune he fancied to learn, eventually embellishing with chords and arpeggios. Although he couldn't sight read well, he played so expressively and musically, many considered him an accomplished musician. Indeed, Lillian loved to hear him play.

Joel opened the cover of the Steinway concert grand piano, revealing the eighty-eight neglected black and white keys beneath. As he sat before the piano on the hard piano stool, the bench creaked. He tinkled out a small tune with two fingers, but soon began to play with both hands.

It had been a long time, but his hands seemed to find their way over the keys, as he played *Moonlight in Vermont*. He was rusty, making some mistakes, but he surprised himself with how well he managed to remember a song he hadn't played in years. After about sixteen measures, he changed his mood, and he played *All You Need Is Love* by the Beatles, bouncing his left hand with the pop bass line.

He envisioned the ghost of Elsa, dancing in front of the piano in a loose, floor-length nightdress, twirling in circles to the music and smiling. The two were entertaining Lillian as she sat on the leather sofa across from the piano, which was perched directly before the wall of books. Lillian sat at the edge of the sofa, laughing at Elsa's silly dance, while she tapped out the song on the floor with her wooden cane. Lillian looked gaunt, week, and unwell, but the two of them managed to grasp hands and laugh, singing and smiling at each other. "All you need is love, love—Love is all you need." Joel would play and sing the "Love is all you need" echoes, answering musically with a high pitched voice. Although Joel could sing well, he sang purposely off-key for comic relief. Elsa, holding Lillian's hands, swayed back and forth in front of Lillian, who sat seated on the couch, and they pretended to dance.

Joel rose from the piano, while they all continued singing. He moved around front to Elsa, and danced with her, pulled her close, twirled her, and then dipped her. As the singing ended, Lillian clapped. "Bravo!" she cried. Joel brought Elsa up from her final dip, and kissed her passionately. They all smiled and laughed.

Even during bleak times, Joel thought, the three of them enjoyed each other's company. Sitting at the piano, he smiled to himself.

Then, Joel suddenly felt overcome with sadness at the realization of what his life had become. His hands were hovering over the keys, and he had stopped playing.

Chapter 6- Restoration of the Estate

Today, unlike other days, Joel did not wake from his slumber on the living room couch on his own accord. Instead, he woke to the loud sound of banging hammers which seemed to emanate from the roof and echo throughout his enormous home. Almost in a stupor, he rose from the couch and walked out the front door, checking his watch as he ventured outside. *Eight o'clock? Really? Seriously?*

Although it wasn't really an ungodly hour at which to start noisy construction, Joel was annoyed to be so rudely awakened, nonetheless. He walked out to the midpoint of the driveway, turning back toward the house. He saw that a group of workers were located on the roof, nailing and re-shingling. The sound of multiple hammers banged out an unsynchronized rhythm.

Just then, Stan approached Joel, tapping him on the shoulder. "I am almost through with the rose garden, Doctor Russell. Would you like to take a look?"

Joel walked out around the far end of the house to find Lillian's old rose garden, brilliantly restored. *She took such pride in this place*, he thought. She and Elsa would sit out on the concrete bench under the apple tree, spending time together reading and talking.

As he approached the bench, he tried to imagine how the young Elsa, seated next to her mother, would appear sharing those precious moments together.

He remembered watching Elsa and Lillian the day they shared one last moment in the garden, seated next to each other on the bench. Lillian had been unsuccessfully battling cancer for some time, and her prognosis wasn't good. That day, she barely had the energy to make the trip from her bed to the bench, but she finally managed to with Elsa's assistance. Lillian wore a heavy robe and slippers. She was now com-pletely bald from an unsuccessful course of chemotherapy.

Elsa leaned her head against her mother's shoul-der, sobbing. Joel stood behind the two watching them share their intimate moment and trying not to intrude. "What am I going to do without you, Momma? It will be just me when you're gone...."

Joel, hearing Elsa's words, did not take offense. He knew what she meant. He noticed, too, that Elsa had called Lillian "Momma", which was the first and only time Elsa called her that. She always referred to Lillian as "Mother".

"Don't be silly, Daughter." Lillian often referred to Elsa simply as "Daughter." "You have Joel! Long after I am dead and buried, you will be making love like bunnies and making me lots and lots of grandchildren!" Lillian turned Elsa's chin and gazed into her weeping face. "Right?"

"Yes, Momma," Elsa replied.

Lillian took great pride in this rose garden. She spent many hours out there pruning, growing, and grafting. Joel remembered what a gifted gardener she was. After her death, Elsa hired a gardener to care for the garden, and she would often go to sit on the bench in somber reflection.

Joel stood over the concrete bench under the apple tree. The seat had a tiled mosaic pattern with the phrase, "Great discoveries have been made while simply lazing under an apple tree." He sat down and looked out at the revived rose garden and contemplated his last conversation with Elsa, while seated there.

Elsa worked diligently to remain fit. Her morning regimen included running five miles through the affluent neighborhood of Ladue. That particular morning, she dressed in workout pants and a sports shirt, wearing a white pair of size seven Reeboks, with her hair tied in a ponytail. She clipped her Sony Walkman, complete with her last mix tape, onto her pant waist, placed her headphones on her head, and headed out the front door.

But this morning he noticed that she was upset and very quiet, and Joel knew that she was trying to conceal it from him. Although they had been trying to have children for almost ten years, Joel and Elsa had recently learned that she could not have children. The news devastated Elsa, and Joel knew she needed comforting. He followed her out the front door. But, both out of shape and dressed in business clothes, he was not able to keep up with her.

"Elsa, wait!" He pleaded. "Stop, please!"

He wasn't sure she had heard him, so he pleaded again, "Please, Elsa. I can't keep up, and I want to talk to you. Come, let's sit down."

They found their way around to the rose garden and sat down next to each other on the concrete bench. Joel put his arm around Elsa's waist.

"You know, this garden meant the world to my mother. We would come here, sit, and talk for hours." Elsa told him.

She paused for a moment. "My mother and I were really close, but my dad and me—not so. He died when I was ten." She paused again. "Joel, do you know what happens to souls when they die?"

"I'm not sure," Joel answered. Neither one of them had been very religious, but Elsa's family did attend church on occasion. "I have often had patients ask me that, especially the depressed and suicidal ones. I tell them honestly that I don't know what happens to us when we die. Of course, they're usually suffering, and they believe that life after death 'couldn't possibly be any worse than living'. I usually tell them, 'But you really don't know, do you? It could be *worse* than living.'"

"It's funny," Elsa continued. "You know, all I remember of my mother and father when they were alive was that they fought constantly. Mother always bitched about him. 'Do you know what your father did today?' she would ask me sometimes. I mean, I was six at the time. I didn't know what he did. I didn't really know him *at all* during my lifetime. But then he died, and Mother's demeanor changed completely. She would visit his grave, and she would meticulously scrape the moss off his headstone. She would talk to him, and she pretended that their life together and their marriage had always been wonderful. It was as though she thought his spirit hovered above her, and he listened to her every word, watching everything she did."

Joel discussed his latest hobby. "You know, I've been reading about Houdini. It's interesting. He was a master illusionist and very close to his mother. After his mother died, he made it his mission to debunk every spiritualist he met who claimed to talk with her. So he and his wife, Bess, had a code word. If Houdini died, he would try to contact Bess. And if anyone came to Bess claiming to have talked to him, she would know that Houdini was truly speaking to her, if he used this code word."

"What was the code word?"

"Rosabelle, BELIEVE", Joel answered.

"So, then what happened?"

"Houdini died, and people tried to contact Bess, but they never managed to use their secret code word. She knew it wasn't him."

"So, let's make a pact, Joel—our own 'Harry and Bess' code."

"What should we use?" Joel asked.

"Let's see. If you think about it, it's like you're heading down a dark coal mine, and you can't see what lies ahead. So you bring a canary. If you're about to be asphyxiated by toxic methane fumes, the canary dies. If everything is okay, the canary lives."

Joel repeated the phrases. "'The canary dies' or 'the canary lives'. Agreed. So now, let's not talk about death. You've got a few good years of life ahead of you before you start to sag and droop. I plan on growing old with you Elsa. Tell me—why are you so obsessed with death all of the sudden?"

"Perhaps it is because I can't have children. Maybe it is that people are less concerned with death if they have children to survive and carry on the family legacy. Isn't that what life is all about, Joel?"

"I can't really say, Elsa. But I can tell you this." He looked directly into her eyes. "My life began the day I spotted you at that party. You lit up the room. I love you, Elsa, and I want to spend the rest of my life with you. I don't know what I would do if I lost you. You mean everything to me, and I want to be with you wherever I am, for as long as I can."

"Yes, Doctor Russell. You always did know the right thing to say." Elsa tried to lighten the mood a little. "By the way, I've also noticed a bit of gray coming in here at your temples." She caressed his receding hairline.

Elsa suddenly turned somber again. "But what about kids, Joel?"

"We'll just keep practicing until we get it right." He sneered, nibbled at Elsa's neck, and tried to tickle her.

As Joel made exaggerated munching noises about her neck, Elsa cackled like a young school girl.

Chapter 7- "Physician, Heal Thyself"

It had been some time—perhaps six months—since Dr. Russell had paid a visit to his primary care physician, Raminder Singh. Although Raminder treated Joel, he also regarded Joel as a colleague, even though Raminder was almost 30 years Joel's junior.

Raminder was an internal medicine resident at Washington University, originally born and raised in India. He was a tall and fit man with a dark complexion. He had a very broad smile, nose and brow. He kept his naturally wavy black hair closely cropped in a very short cut, to keep it under control and looking professional.

Joel remarked that he had selected Dr. Singh as a primary care physician because he had an amazing memory. Although he reported here for his annual physical, he was more interested in getting Raminder to write him a script for another six month supply of Zoloft.

"I heard about Jake Sternen, Joel. How are you holding up?" Raminder asked.

"I'm not too concerned. I doubt he is in the area. And, even if he poses a threat to me, I don't particularly care."

Joel's apathetic tone caused Raminder to look even more concerned. "Joel, you look like hell. We need to talk about your moving on with your life. Start seeing patients. Get yourself a project of some kind. It has been seven years since all this has happened." Doctor Singh had a very thick Eastern Indian accent. He spoke Hindi, as Joel recalled, and immigrated to America with his new wife a year or two after 9/11. He moved from Cambridge to St. Louis in 2006, when he started his residency at Wash U. (Joel noted how, when Raminder said the word "we", he heard the underlying "vwe" sound, typical of his thick accent.)

"Have you thought about starting to see patients again?" Raminder asked.

"Well, I'm actually in the midst of trying to sell Elsa's house." He referred to it once more as *Elsa's house*. "I have thought about perhaps working here with outreach patients. And I am considering starting a social network—a kind of support system—for the mentally ill. You know—support groups for patients and loved ones, information on meetings, latest developments in treatment, information on resources and physicians, and the like—complete with blogs and threads designed to help mentally ill patients. I've got to think through the logistics of availability for the patients and obvious privacy issues. Although many people have access to the internet, those who are homeless and who are in the grips of poverty still don't have those technologies available, unless they go to the public library. And of course, my area of

52

expertise is psychiatry. I would have to hire an expert in the computer science field in order to help me plan the project."

"Really?" Raminder asked. "What kind of expert?"

"A systems analyst. Pretty much, I would have to rely on that expert to take these ideas I have and help them come to fruition. So, I would need a software *and* hardware expert. I would be willing to fund the whole project, but I would have to find someone who understands the technologies we have on hand today, help adapt them to our current needs, give me an estimate on what the project would cost, and help follow through with the initial implementation of the project. Once the project had been launched, we could hire someone else to come in and maintain it."

"Really?" Raminder, looking interested, paused for a moment. "You know, we just found out that my wife, Priya, is now pregnant. You've never met her, but we married in India before we both went to Massachusetts. She went to MIT, and I finished up my degree at Harvard. She has just now finished her master's thesis at Washington University. I believe that she might be just the person you might need for this job. We are actually trying to find her an interim project to get involved in before the baby arrives. Hopefully, we can pay down some of our student loans and put some money away before the baby is born. And my residency will be through here shortly. After that, we had hoped to go back to India to visit. She is very homesick."

"Do you think she would be interested in helping out? I have no doubt that she is capable, but my plans are sketchy, at best."

"Joel, I think you should call her. Here is her number, and I will give her a heads up that you will be calling."

"So you met in India?"

"Yes. Through shaadi.com. It's sort of a 'match.com', big in India. It's more of a modern day version of prearranged marriages. You kind of screen your potential spouse online, then a matchmaker and families get involved in the marriage process. She is a very intelligent and beautiful woman, Joel. I am very happy."

"I'm glad to hear that, Raminder. I look forward to meeting her."

Chapter 8- The Sale of the Elsa's Estate

When Ellen Rodriguez broke the news to Joel of his pending estate sale, she seemed giddy with excitement. Her business as a realtor had tanked since the real estate bubble burst, and this was her first big, successful sale in a long time. She was so giddy that she bounced up and down and squealed like a teenage girl with a crush, who had just caught a glimpse of her favorite movie star. Although she was clearly middle-aged, her shape was still pleasing. Her generous cleavage struggled to contain itself in a precariously tight-fitting tank top. Joel noted that Ellen often looked as though she shopped in the juniors' sections of the expensive department stores, because she usually dressed like a teenager. He also noted, by the delayed way in which her breasts bounced, that he was fairly sure her bosoms were fake.

"We have a couple who wants to buy this estate for 2.75 mill *as is!*" Ellen exclaimed to Joel.

"As is?" Joel asked. He looked across the room at his possessions stacked in boxes which reached up to the ceiling.

"Well, of course, you still need to get your crap outta here, Joel. Oh my God, I am so excited! This is so great for me! I'll let you know the rest of the details later." She hugged Joel, turned, and ran out of the house, not even waiting for a response or consent to the sale. Joel just stood there in his living room before piles of boxes, speechless and amazed.

Joel managed to hire a small moving company to move his boxes and select belongings to a small home he rented in Dogtown, in downtown South Saint Louis, close to both Washington and Saint Louis Universities. Although he could have easily afforded a home in the more affluent neighborhoods of the Central West End, he felt more comfortable on this side of Highway 40. These people were a little more down to earth, and he could breathe here. The landlord would even permit pets, should Joel decide to ever make the commitment and adopt one. *Perhaps I should get a dog or something*, Joel thought to himself briefly. And then, when he considered the extent of commitment being a pet owner would entail, he thought of it no more.

The possessions Joel managed to take with him consisted of the box of belongings Joanna had given to him when she cleared out his office, some of the wedding photos and memorabilia Elsa had kept through the years, the living room sofa he had managed to make a bed of over the last seven years, the dusty coffee table, a bookcase, complete with some staple psychiatric books such as the *Diagnostic Statistical Manual* and his Houdini books, and some cookware for the kitchen. The rest of the items were discarded, auctioned, or donated, or left as bonus furnishings for the new owners of Elsa's estate. He did not have a bed or a TV. Although he probably would have loved to keep Lillian's piano, he decided there wasn't a sufficient amount of room for such a monstrosity to make it through the front door of his tiny house. So, he decided instead to leave it as a gift in the old den for the new owners.

Aside from these bare furnishings, Joel's Dogtown rental wasn't all that bad. Like most of the houses in older South Saint Louis, it had an unassuming brick exterior, reportedly built during the Craftsman era. The house was obviously old, but it was solidly constructed. The rooms were still admittedly small. *Enough space for one*, Joel thought. *I just need a place to crash.*

He decided that he missed living downtown. The Ladue estate was in close proximity to the city but far enough from the bustle of downtown that, at times, Joel felt isolated. Of course, during the recent past, he *desired* that isolation. But now, he desired to purge himself of the past and move on. *No, this place is good*, he affirmed. *This will do nicely.*

The old Lemp Brewery consisted of a bunch of warehouses stretching several city blocks south of the current Anheuser-Busch Brewery. Initially, the Lemp Brewery achieved more success than its famous competitor, being the most successful Saint Louis brewer prior to the establishment of Prohibition.

Unfortunately, after the repeal of Prohibition, the family failed in their attempts to revive the business.

The brewery was established by Adam Lemp, a German immigrant who came to the U.S. during the early 1800s, bringing with him the skills he had acquired in the Fatherland for making German lager. Soon, due to the influx of a widely German population of Saint Louis immigrants, his beer was in high demand. His lager appealed to the German palate and lifestyle. His heirs managed to expand the business, which then established the Lemps as one of the wealthiest families in Saint Louis.

The brewery was originally built over a system of underground caves, stretching over the span of eleven city blocks all the way to the Mississippi Riverfront. The caves facilitated the primary and secondary fermentation processes required for production of the lager prior to the age of refrigeration. As time progressed and the Lemp lager business grew, William Lemp, Senior constructed the brewery warehouses above this underground system of caves. The family lived in a mansion acquired in 1860, just north of the breweries and cave system, on the street now commonly known as DeMenil Place.

The Lemp family did not experience success without more than its share of tragedy, however. In 1902, the distraught William Lemp, Sr. shot himself in the DeMenil mansion. Later in 1920, William's daughter, Elsa Lemp, committed suicide in her Saint Louis home, although questions were raised as to whether Elsa's suicide was truly a suicide or a homicide. In 1922, again in the DeMenil mansion, William Lemp, Jr. shot himself. Finally, an old and frail Charles Lemp committed suicide in the mansion in 1949.

Three of these family suicides were reported to have occurred in the Lemp family mansion, which was located just north of the brewery warehouses. The mansion, adjacent brewery warehouses, and what remained of the cave system beneath were reported to be a hotbed of paranormal activity, and the subject of many national ghost-hunting documentaries.

The warehouses in the old brewery were being leased for different reasons. But the warehouse adjacent to Cherokee Street, just across from the DeMenil mansion, was being leased room by room, mostly to struggling bands and musicians. These rooms functioned as the ideal practice rooms for bands, who tended to be very loud at times. In this older neighborhood—admittedly now a questionable area of town—loud noises were the least of the neighborhood's concerns. Clearly, neighborhoods in the adjacent blocks had more pressing safety issues at hand, including impending problems with gang activity, drug-related shootings, and high crime rates.

It was in this particular warehouse that Ariel and her band had chosen to rent a practice room. After extending an invitation to Joel to visit her there, Ariel offered to give Joel a tour of the facility. On this particular evening, she met him outside after work. It was now dusk, and her band had assembled for their weekly practice session.

"I have to let you in. Can't get in unless you have a key." Ariel fiddled with her massive, custodial-sized key chain, trying to find the correct key. Finally managing to find the right one, she opened the door and showed Joel into the warehouse. He could hear electric guitars blaring from the rooms upstairs.

The flooring of the old warehouse creaked as they ascended the stairs. At the top, a series of doors stretched down the hallway on either side, leading into separate practice rooms for each different band. At certain points in the hallway, there were open areas, where there would be a sofa, sitting area, or bar, where lessees would loiter when they weren't actually practicing in their rooms. The white walls were adorned with original murals, one of which was a black and white mural depicting famous celebrities, both living and deceased.

Ariel showed Joel into her practice room, where the band members had now congregated. Studio and musical equipment lined each available wall, and a drum set had been assembled near the room's entrance. She introduced Joel to the four other members of her band—one drummer, two guitarists, and a bass player. Ariel sang lead vocals and played keyboard. She introduced the drummer, Aaron, as her boyfriend and then greeted him with a kiss. He was a nice looking young man in his late twenties. Joel concluded from the way that Aaron dressed that he must have had a "day job".

The bass player, Bruce, struck Joel as a bit odd, even for a musician. He was friendly, wearing Bermuda shorts and a black, Nirvana t-shirt, smoking a cigarette, and sporting a long ponytail. At first, he seemed preoccupied, but Joel soon realized he had been toking a little too heavily on reefer.

Joel also noticed Ariel's small electronic keyboard in the room. At first begging permission, he sat down and played an improvised version of Adele's *Someone Like You*. Ariel and the others stood amazed. She sang with him.

"Dr. Russell, I had no idea you played," Ariel stated, surprised.

"Me neither," he joked. "At least I've never played *this* song before—only heard it on the radio. By the way, Ariel, call me Joel. You don't work for me anymore, and I'm not really doctoring anymore either." Joel managed to carry on this conversation while continuing to play. "Maybe I should start my own band and rent out a space here for myself. Sort of a post, mid-life career change…"

"Seriously?" Ariel replied. I can introduce you to the landlord. I think there are a couple of free rooms—people who just got kicked out because they didn't pay the rent. And the entire third floor is vacant. But, I have to warn you…." She hesitated. "There are some spooky things that go on here. And parking is a bitch during the entire month of October."

Ariel and the other band members suddenly looked very serious.

Interested, Joel stopped playing. "Like what? Ghosts?"

"The Lavender Lady," whispered Bruce secretively, as if someone present might take offense.

During the early 1900s, William Lemp, Jr. had been married to Lillian Hanlan in a reportedly "mixed" marriage of sorts. His family was Lutheran, and her family was Roman Catholic. Although their only son William Lemp, III was born of this marriage, theirs was a rocky marriage at best. Their union finally ended in a scandalous divorce trial shortly after the turn of the century. William Lemp, Jr. had stated during the trial that he was embarrassed by Lillian's flamboyance. Many in Saint Louis Society claimed that she insisted on wearing only lavender, which made her a conspicuous public figure. It was reported that William Lemp, Jr. himself coined the term, "Lavender Lady" in reference to his estranged wife—an intentionally derogatory nickname which had stuck to the present day.

"Dude, there is some freaky-ass shit that goes on here when nobody is around," added one of the guitarists.

"Really?" Joel was now completely engaged.

"Yeah—doors slamming, lights flicker on and off all the time—that kind of crap. One time—I think it was about 3 A.M., I was recording vocals on my computer here, all alone in the place. And when I played it back, I could hear voices in the background. Dude, there wasn't a soul around, but I could clearly pick out strange voices on the audio when I wasn't singing. I couldn't make out what they were saying, and I had to turn it up real loud." The guitarist acted this all out for Joel and continued. "It almost sounded like German....very freaky!" The guitarist related this entire story while holding his cigarette. Joel noted that he needed an ash tray, because his ashes were growing long and were about to fall on the floor.

Joel also noticed that Ariel suddenly turned white. "What's wrong?" he asked as he turned to her.

She sat down and carefully considered her response. "I know everybody thinks I'm nuts, but *I see dead people.*"

"Yeah, like that little dude in that movie with Bruce Willis," the second guitarist joked.

"No, I'm serious. I get these strange feelings that come over me, like I'm being watched—like there is somebody here watching me. And not just the Lavender Lady, but other people. People I don't know and who don't know me. Sometimes it's like I can almost see them, they are so real. I see them in my dreams. Really, I only fell asleep here once, and I had the freakiest dream....." Ariel hesitated again.

Although she had discussed this dream with Aaron and the rest of the band, she hesitated because of Joel's presence. Joel figured that she feared discussing it with him. But her ambivalence about recounting the dream wasn't because Joel was a shrink. It was something else.

Joel tried to allay Ariel's fears and encouraged her to speak up. "They're just dreams," he assured.

"Well," Ariel began slowly. "I started falling asleep on this couch. I had a long day, and we just finished practice, but I was even too tired to drive home. I was like sort of drifting off into sleep, and I could hear these voices. I was floating around, watching this place come to life. I was moving through the rooms—you know—still kind of floating. And I could see all these men, moving around. Like it was 100 years ago and everybody's around just making beer. Nobody was paying attention to me, as I moved from room to room.

"I walked out into the street towards the mansion, and I could see this well-dressed man with gray hair and a full beard and mustache, walking up and down the street, very upset. He just kept pacing back and forth, like he was very disturbed about something. He almost looked like he was half-crazed with grief.

"Then, it seemed like I was floating toward the mansion. There were people downstairs, dancing. There was some kind of wild party going on. Women, half-naked, romping around and men, drinking. In the middle of all this, there was another well-dressed man in a gray suit who sees me. In fact, he was the only one in my dream who actually noticed my presence. Everybody else didn't seem to notice me at all. It was as if *I* was the spirit, and *they* were real. So the man looks me in the eye and says, 'Elsa didn't shoot herself. Somebody murdered her!' He pointed behind me, and I turned around. But—"

"But what?" Joel motioned her to continue.

"It wasn't Elsa *Lemp* standing behind me. It was another Elsa......it was *your* Elsa, Joel." Ariel paused for a reaction from Joel. She continued, "Then, Elsa smiled at me and walked up to me. She tapped me on the shoulder, and said something really strange. She said...."

"Yes?"

"She said, 'Tell Mr. Houdini that Bess is here, waiting.' Just then, I woke up, sweating through my clothes. I felt Elsa's presence in the room. I thought I could even smell the scent of her perfume, but I was by myself. I jumped up, grabbed my car keys and ran the hell out of here!"

Joel sat dumbfounded.

"Really, Doctor Russell—" she immediately corrected herself, "—uh, Joel...I know you think I'm crazy when I say that, but it scared the living shit out of me! That was the first and only time I slept here, and I won't ever do that again! I won't even let Aaron leave me here by myself anymore. I guess you could say I've had this kind of stuff happen all my life—you know, premonitions and dreams about junk—but here it's *way worse*. It's all over this place! And it's not just me—other people have said the same types of things have happened to them."

She looked at Joel and shrugged her shoulders. "What?" she asked, almost expecting him to say he thought she was nuts.

Joel nodded his head from side to side. "Just thinking..." he replied. He pursed his lips as he smiled.

Chapter 9- The Loss of Elsa

The Forest Park Garage off Forest Park Parkway was not on Dr. Russell's way home from the old brew houses to his Dogtown rental. But tonight, he decided to take a detour. After his conversation with Ariel, he was bewildered. During the three years prior to her death, Elsa was like a mother to Ariel, and the two became very close. It disturbed him to see how shaken Ariel had been recounting her dream. He realized how difficult it was for her as a young woman to come to grips with the circumstances of Elsa's death. It was truly a difficult thing for *everyone* who loved Elsa to come to grips with the tragedy of her death.

But what puzzled Joel about Ariel's dream was that Ariel didn't seem to comprehend the significance of Elsa's references to Houdini and Bess.

Dr. Russell was, first and foremost, a scientist. But in recent years, he doubted his once firmly established scientific notions. He never really believed in ghosts. The handful of times he might have naïvely interpreted some sign or some occurrence as supernatural, he often explained it away logically, as most scientists would. Ariel was aware that Joel had a fascination with reading about Houdini, but she didn't really know much about the magician herself. And Ariel was a honest woman who respected Joel, so it was unlikely that she would just make the whole thing up.

Driving by the parking garage, Joel noted that there were no signs of what had taken place there seven years earlier. *How could this building's former scars have been so quickly healed? How could everyone and everyone have moved on,* he thought, *and yet I still seem to be stuck here?*

Joel parked his car at a vacant meter off the parkway, leaving it running. He stared toward the front of the garage, remembering the events which occurred only seven years before.

It was June 2003, and Dr. Russell had arrived at an appreciation dinner for patrons of the Siteman Cancer Center and Center for Advanced Medicine. He and Elsa, along with several other affluent patrons, were guests of honor, having donated sizeable sums for cancer research. The dinner was being held at the Chase Park Plaza Hotel, few blocks north of the North Campus of Barnes-Jewish Hospital.

The Center for Advanced Medicine was a state-of-the-art facility completed in 2001, which promised to bring in ground-breaking treatment and technologies to those suffering from cancer. Joel planned to meet Elsa, who was already in attendance at the hotel, having previously taken a cab there. Although Joel and Elsa contributed to many causes throughout the city, this particular honor meant a great deal to Elsa, because she donated this gift in memory of her mother Lillian, who had passed away from cancer more than fifteen years earlier.

Joel parked his black Lexus in the parking garage and made his way to the hotel. He did not like to use valet parking, because he was very touchy about his car. But really, he just preferred to remain as anonymously inconspicuous as possible. Even though he was married to a socialite, he preferred to park his own car instead of drawing any special attention to himself by using a valet.

He arrived in the lobby of the luxury hotel where Elsa greeted him. She, of course, introduced him to her many influential acquaintances. But it had been some time since Joel worked downtown, and he seemed unacquainted with most of the new physicians now practicing at the university. So, while Elsa "flitted"—which is what Elsa did best—Joel sat it out, as usual, just observing the crowd.

Joanna Watson and other physicians from Joel's practice were in attendance. Everyone had dressed to the nines, since this was a black tie benefit. Joanna glanced over at Joel from time to time, but other than saying an initial "Hello", made no attempt to engage him or her colleagues in polite conversation. Elsa continued to flit about and seemed to have forgotten about Joel.

During the benefit, Joel became engrossed in thought. He thought about his and Elsa's relationship and how they seemed to grow apart during the past few years. We have *been married to each other twenty-one years*, he thought. *Every relationship progresses from romantic to companionate at some point in time. Surely, we have done well to stay together this long.* He looked over at Joanna—a young, intelligent beauty, attracted to him and full of passion. *She is at my command and would do whatever I ask of her.* Then he glanced back at Elsa. *Twenty years older, and she is still the beautiful woman I married. True, she is her own woman. She **owns** this event, and I am merely a spectator. But somehow, she manages to love me in spite of how despicable I am.*

Suddenly realizing the extent of his deception of Elsa and how deeply involved he had become with Joanna, Joel felt sick and made his way to the men's room. On his way there, he seemed to be so self-absorbed that he didn't notice that Joanna had followed him. He entered the men's room, making his way into a booth. Joanna followed him in, pushing him in, and locking the door behind her. Joel could tell that she had drunk too much champagne.

"Doesn't the thought of potentially being caught just turn you on?" she asked, grabbing his waist and pulling his crotch to rub against hers. "Let's do it right here." She nibbled at his neck while simultaneously trying to pull off his bow tie.

Joanna wore a scarlet, floor-length gown, with a huge slit up the left side. She kissed him deeply on the lips, and he breathed heavily. She inserted his right palm into the slit in her skirt and ran his hand up the outside of her thigh. "I came commando," she warned, revealing only stockings and a garter beneath.

Joel was overcome with desire and felt himself becoming erect. It had been several weeks since he and Joanna had an opportunity to be together—even longer for him and Elsa—and he was overdue for some good, old-fashioned sexual release.

Then, Joel stopped. He pulled back. "Joanna, I can't."

"What?" she continued to nibble at his neck again. "It's just sex, Joel." This time she tried to unhook his cummerbund.

"No," Joel pulled her off his neck and look directly into her eyes. "I can't do this anymore—to you or Elsa. I can't keep hurting people I care about."

Joanna stopped. This was the first time Joel ever rejected her advances. He was not the type to play games. She knew that he was serious—not just about resisting her that evening. He was trying to break their affair off completely.

Tears welled up in her eyes. "But, Joel—I love you."

This was the first time Joanna ever admitted to being in love with Joel. He had suspected that she was in love with him for some time, but until now, she never admitted it. He carried on this relationship with her in almost a state of denial. *As long as she doesn't admit she loves me, I won't be hurting her,* he naïvely tried to convince himself.

"No, Joanna. We have to stop. We can't go on doing this. There is no future for you with me. Elsa is my wife, and I love her."

She understood that he *was* serious. Joel had never before mentioned breaking off their affair. She began to tremble. The tears were flowing now even more fiercely, and her whimpering was now audible. The men's room was empty except for the two of them, but Joel feared that someone would come in at any minute and discover the two of them together.

"I'm sorry, Joanna. I can't be for you the man you need me to be." He held her chin and looked deeply into her tortured eyes. "You need someone to love you for the drop-dead, gorgeous, intelligent knock-out you are. Someone who can devote the rest of his long life with you. I can't do that for you. I'm not that guy. I love Elsa, and I've neglected her for far too long."

For about a minute, Joanna stood looking at Joel, dumbstruck. Then, she pulled his hand away, looking down and moving back. She unlocked the door to the men's room booth, letting herself out. "I have to go now." She stumbled out the men's room exit and stood in the hallway rearranging herself before heading off. All the while, she made futile attempts to fight back the tears which seemed only to flow even faster and more furiously.

Minutes before, Elsa had notice that Joel had been missing from the benefit. She began to search for him. She thought, perhaps, she might track him down near the men's room. When she turned the corner to look for him, she spotted the visibly upset Joanna, exiting the men's room and moving off in the opposite direction. In her despair, Joanna didn't notice Elsa at all.

Elsa stood for a moment in the hallway, trying to process what she had just witnessed. Still, it hadn't occurred to her that Joanna and Joel had been together. But then, moments later, Joel exited the men's room to witness Elsa standing there. And now, she realized what had actually gone on between her husband and his young and beautiful colleague.

Joel was a skilled psychiatrist and able to read people quite well. When he saw Elsa standing there speechless—the woman who never lost her composure—he read her transparently. He understood that she now discovered the secret of his betrayal. He had hoped that, in choosing to end his affair with Joanna, he could take this secret to his grave and spare Elsa any undue pain. But there she stood. And Joel knew, just by reading her expression, that she had figured out everything that he had been hiding from her for the past year.

"Elsa, I can explain...." Joel approached her, but she cringed, still speechless. Elsa held up her hands as if to shield herself from the anticipated onslaught of excuses. Then, she turned to run.

"No, Elsa, please stop!" Joel cried.

She wouldn't listen. She hurriedly headed out through the large revolving doors, past the valet parking, south to the Forest Park Garage. She ran quickly, darting across the street, dodging oncoming traffic through the intersection out toward the parking garage. Even though Elsa was both fumbling for car keys and wearing high heels, her years of morning runs still made her faster than her out-of-shape husband. Joel couldn't keep up. He called to her again, "Elsa, please wait! Elsa!"

Despite his pleas, she had left him far behind. Joel hadn't the stamina to keep up. He stopped at the street corner to catch his breath. He leaned down, gasping for breath for what seemed like three or four minutes. Then, a horrendous explosion went off in the parking garage on the floor on which Joel had parked the Lexus. *Oh my God—Elsa! Something has happened to her!*

Joel felt propelled by extraordinary forces across the street and up two flights of stairs to the third floor of the parking garage. It was then he realized his worst fears. Flames had now consumed the Lexus, also engulfing several vehicles on either side of his car. And inside, he knew—now surely dead—was his beloved Elsa.

Joel stood, both hysterical and in shock, amidst the chaos of the explosion which had previously ripped through the garage. He froze with fear. He couldn't move. He could only watch in horror as the only woman he ever truly loved was ripped from him.

Through the rising smoke and flames, Joel noticed another figure across the garage in the distance. This man also stood frozen in horror, looking back at him. The man was Jake Sternen, a former patient of Joel's who had recently been hospitalized and had threatened Joel's life. When Jake realized that Dr. Russell had recognized him, he came to his senses and ran off.

After contemplating the events immediately leading up to Elsa's death, Joel put his car in gear, pulled out of his parking space, and wound his car around Kingshighway to head South to his Dogtown rental home.

That should have been me, he thought. *I should have died that night—not Elsa. I wish I had died that night.*

Chapter 10- The New Bed

When Joel answered his door at 3 P.M., a uniformed man in shorts stood before him. "Are you Doctor Russell?" he inquired.

Joel nodded.

"Uh, we're here to deliver your new bed?" The young man was making a statement, but he posed it like a question to Joel, who confirmed that he was delivering to the correct home. He directed the young man and his coworker up the stairs to his empty bedroom, where he instructed them to assemble the bed.

The new bed was nothing special. Joel had sold the massive king-sized bed formerly belonging to him and Elsa at the Ladue house. He hadn't slept in the bed since Elsa died. The bed was too depressing and spacious and still smelled of her. Her unoccupied side only served as a constant reminder of what he had lost. That is why he spent the next seven years sleeping on the living room sofa, now too worn to be used as a bed. In addition, his back could no longer take the restless nights and having to wake up sore all the time. He was far too old for that nonsense.

This new bed was a full-sized bed, with a fairly standard, contemporary hardwood headboard and frame. When he tested the mattress at the mattress store, it felt comfortable, but yet not as enormous as his old king.

The two delivery men quickly assembled the bed for Joel, who tipped them each a twenty dollar bill and thanked them for their efforts.

That night, he unwrapped a brand new set of sheets he bought at a department store and made his new bed. He didn't wash the sheets first; he just made the bed. Since it was getting colder, he had purchased a matching down comforter and laid it across the bed.

He undressed down to his boxers and slipped beneath the covers. The brand new sheets were still crisp with sizing, but still much more comfortable than what Joel had been accustomed to sleeping in. Perhaps he hadn't treated himself to a comfortable bed all these years, because he thought he didn't deserve comfort. *Perhaps*, he decided, *it would be better for me to try to overcome my self-depriving behavior of the past seven years. Maybe I have punished myself enough for my past transgressions.*

He sensed a new awareness of his warm, new comforter. He felt the crispness of the new sheets and the softness of the bed against his bare skin and worn body. And, for the first time in longer than he could remember, he suddenly became aware of himself.

In the darkness, he closed his eyes and remembered Elsa's warmth and softness. How sweetly she smelled. What fragrance did she wear? That's right—

Lauren. She always smelled so clean. He loved her smell. And, as he stroked himself to a climax, dreaming of beautiful wife, he thought of the many intimate moments they shared together during their twenty-one year marriage.

How he missed her softness, her warmth, her beauty, her wit, and her gentle smile. How he longed to be with her once again and tell her how truly sorry he was for breaking her heart. He wanted her to forgive him for all his past indiscretions with Joanna. He wanted to take it all back and remember his last glimpse of her with that unconditionally loving and accepting smile she always gave him.

Instead, he could only recall his final memory of her last expression—that look of disappointment and betrayal.

Joel turned over in his crisp new bed, nestled under the warmth of the down comforter, and cried himself to sleep.

Chapter 11- The Meeting with Priya

The Lemp Mansion on DeMenil had fallen into disrepair after the suicide of Charles in 1949, and for about twenty years, it operated as a "flophouse". During the late 1970s, the Porter family purchased the house for a paltry sum. They renovated it and turned into a bed and breakfast.

This evening, the restaurant opened promptly at 5:30 P.M., and Joel had reservations to meet Raminder's wife, Priya, to discuss his project plans. He carried a large messenger bag with him. The maître d' sat him at a private table, while he awaited Mrs. Singh's arrival.

When Priya arrived a few minutes later, she greeted Joel as he stood to shake her hand. She was a beautiful young Indian woman in her late twenties, with a deep brown complexion, long and silky, jet-black hair, and captivating brown, almond-shaped eyes. She dressed in a silk coral blouse and matching pants, which were accented by ornate gold dots. She also wore a coordinated, sheer emerald scarf, which she draped loosely about her left shoulder. Her long, emerald bead earrings stretched down to the tops of her shoulders and precisely matched the color of her sari. She had an innocent smile, full lips, and perfectly white, straight teeth. Her nose was broad, but perfect in size and shape for her face.

Joel was struck by Priya's natural beauty. He thought she resembled a famous Bollywood actress he had seen in a recent independent film. She was petite in stature and exuded innocence, as if she were completely unaware of her exotic beauty. Although she was clearly glowing, a visible baby bump was not yet apparent. Of course, Joel had to admit—he hadn't looked too carefully, fearing that she might consider his behavior rude.

He pulled her seat out for her. She thanked him and sat. He, in turn, sat down.

"Raminder tells me marvelous things about you, Doctor Russell."

"Please call me Joel. And he also speaks proudly of you and your accomplishments. First, would you like to order? The food is very good here." Priya nodded and picked up a menu.

During dinner, Joel quizzed Priya about her education, her home and family in India, and how she met Raminder. She impressed Joel with the level of respect she exhibited regarding Raminder and his achievements. When she spoke of her own accomplishments, she downplayed them. Joel believed that, even though she was young, she was also an expert in her field.

Priya asked Joel about his life and chosen career. He talked very briefly about the loss of his wife, Elsa. He didn't go into great detail, except to say that he had been married twenty-one years. Priya could sense his uneasiness when discussing Elsa. Raminder had filled her in on some of the details of Elsa's death, so she didn't elicit any additional information regarding Elsa, for fear of upsetting Joel.

When they had finished dinner, Dr. Russell decided to segue into a discussion about his project by bringing up Raminder again. "Raminder feels you might be able to help me with my current distraction—a project I have planned."

"He talked about it briefly. Tell me more about your ideas."

Joel looked at her thoughtfully. "First, tell me, Priya—Do you believe in love?"

"I'm not sure what you mean," she responded, puzzled.

"I mean, do you believe in love? You know, like the love between a man and a woman. Don't you love Raminder?"

"Well, yes. I have grown to love him through the years. I was attracted to him in the beginning, and I have grown to respect him. My family likes him, and I think he will be a wonderful father to my children."

"What about your family? Raminder said you were homesick. Whom do you miss most?" Joel asked.

"My mother."

"She is still living? No doubt you have established a bond with her that has transcended the huge distance between you, since you long so to return to India, no?"

"True."

"I also have no doubt that, once your baby is born, you will share that same bond with him or her—one that transcends even, let's say—death?"

"Well, traditionally Hindus believe in reincarnation."

"I understand that, but isn't there some part of you who thinks that this bond you have with your mother—the one you will undoubtedly have with your first child—will continue to remain, long after you have died?"

"I suppose so."

"Priya, I don't profess to know what happens from beyond the grave. Maybe you're right. But I'd *like* to know."

"I'm not sure I follow."

"Let me put it to you plainly. I would like to hire you to help me communicate with the dead."

Priya looked surprised.

"It does sound crazy, but hear me out. I have an entire floor of rooms in the old brewery, just south of here, in which I intend to set up a computer system. This would function as a unique 'social network', which would eventually enable us to communicate with the dead. Or more likely, the dead to communicate with the living."

Joel motioned around himself. "This entire place is ripe with reports of paranormal activity—here at this house and down there, at the old brewery. I'm not sure what all this energy is, because parapsychology is not my area of expertise. But I believe there are undeniable forces existing all around us. Only here, I believe, this energy is amplified."

Priya looked incredulous. "I misunderstood. Raminder said you were interested in implementing a social network, complete with resources for the mentally ill."

"I lied. Look, Priya. I'm a mental health professional. I know how doctors think. If I told Raminder I intended to hire you to launch a network project to help me talk to dead people, what do you think he would do?"

Priya considered Joel's question for a moment. "Yes, I see your point. But really, Joel, what makes you so sure that I would be both able to help you and also willing to keep this a secret from my husband?"

"I have no doubt that, if anyone can help me with this project, it would be you. As for keeping this project a secret, well—here." Joel picked up his messenger bag and dumped its contents on the table. He revealed an oversized wad of crisp hundred dollar bills, all neatly bundled together. "MIT, Harvard, Wash U—that type of education is not cheap, Priya. Do you really want to start off your new lives as parents indebted in student loans up to your eyeballs? This money would pay off all your loans, Raminder's loans, and set up your baby and any future babies you might have for life. When this project is complete, you and Raminder and Raminder Junior can fly back to India and spend all the time you want to with your mother."

Priya looked tempted but shook her head. "I am not sure I will be able to deliver what you want. I would be stealing your money, if I was not able to accomplish what you needed. I cannot guarantee anything."

"I am only asking for the next eight months of your life to work on this for me." Joel could read the skeptical look in Priya's face. "C'mon, humor me, Priya. I have nothing left in my life to look forward to. This will keep an old man occupied and busy, and you will make a few extra bucks he has to share, helping him relive his lost past. What have you got to lose? Just share a little of your expertise and time."

"It really does sound crazy." Priya paused. "Can I think about it for a couple of days?"

"Sure. In the meantime, why don't I take you on a tour of the warehouse?"

Joel had rented the entire third floor of rooms at the brewery, one floor above Ariel's room. He convinced the landlord to let him knock down the connecting, non load-bearing walls between rooms. And he planned to reinforce, as best as he could, and soundproof all the remaining walls. Joel also talked about extra accommodations he would have to make for all the equipment and the separate power supply he would have to have installed. But he and Priya would need to sit down and determine what type of hardware they would have to purchase. When the landlord seemed suspicious about Joel's project, he gave him the same story he gave to Raminder. Finally, when Joel offered the man five times the standard room rate, with three years paid in cash in advance, the landlord stopped asking any more questions about the project. As a precaution, Joel assured him that there would be no illegal activity occurring on the premises, and the landlord consented. Joel also offered to foot the bill for all capital expenditures made to the rented rooms to accommodate his advanced power and security needs.

The project required a great deal of thought. Since money was not an object, they would have to decide how these "entities" might interface with a computer system in place. Priya had mentioned something about some new game technologies and a type of motion sensor, which had recently been promoted for some newly released computer games on the market. Perhaps, she might adapt them so that they could ultimately sense paranormal activity as movement, enabling spirits to potentially interact with the software.

Then, there was the issue of software develop-ment. How do you make a software program that is ghost-friendly? They would need to write a unique program, employing a ghost-friendly interface. In addition, they would need to hire several programmers to develop this project within such a short time frame.

And finally, there had to be several applications in place for several, choice modes of interaction with the spirit world. EMF detectors had long been used by parapsychologists to sense anomalies in the electromagnetic field and ultimately hunt down ghosts. How could that work for this new project? What about voice recorders? And, if the interface was really ghost-friendly, what was the easiest way to register spirits as users? Perhaps the system could automatically download death records and obituary data from global newspapers on a daily basis, setting up user accounts for the deceased.

These were all considerations which Joel and Priya would need to discuss. And several days later, after considering Joel's offer, Priya agreed to help with the project, which he named Project Séance. They would spend the next eight months hammering out details of hardware requirements, software development, staffing issues, and any hair-brained idea they might decide to implement.

Joel felt excited. Not so much because he might actually be able to talk to Elsa, but because he had something—at least temporarily—to live for. Once she overcame her initial skepticism, Priya considered it a unique challenge, unlike any other project she would be asked to implement again. It was certainly not something she could ever include on her résumé, but it promised to be an interesting diversion for her, just the same. And, because Joel had no unrealistic expectations of success, the worst case scenario was that she had simply wasted some nervous energy and just a few months of her time.

Chapter 12- The Birth of Project Séance

It was time to begin the development of Project Séance. But first Joel and Priya would need to discuss, in detail, their plans on how they would achieve success. They would also need to consider the logistics of how the project was going to operate, how they were going to staff the project, the resources at hand, and what additional resources they needed to procure. They had to develop a timeline of estimated delivery dates.

Ultimately, they had less than eight months to complete this project. Priya intended on being a full-time mother after the baby was born. So, they set her due date as the project completion date, after which time, Priya would relinquish the project operations completely over to Joel. This meant that they would both have to put in a lot of long hours getting the project underway and finished.

It would take a minimum of four weeks to manage all the capital improvements to the new space being rented at the brewery. Joel paid top dollar to ensure that these changes would take place as quickly as humanly possible. This included demolition work to knock down some adjoining walls, reinforcement of the existing walls, installation of a heavy duty door with punch code security clearance access, and new electrical wiring to power all the technologies necessary to run the new project. Joel's operation would have its own breaker box and meter, so that he would be responsible for the extra energy costs associated with maintaining the project.

For this four week period, Priya had taken the time to purchase two new computers and hook up wireless access for Joel in the living room of his Dogtown home. This space would function as their temporary headquarters. They would meet there early each morning to go over their business plans for the day. Priya would give Joel a list of purchases she intended to make for equipment, and he would hand her his credit card in order to acquire the necessary items. Sometimes, if she provided him with an estimate for the day, he would simply pull out a stack of cash and hand it to her. He was not interested in receipts, because this was not a business venture. Joel regarded Project Séance simply as a very expensive hobby.

On one particular day, Joel agreed to meet Priya in front of the Best Buy to look at some equipment. The store had just unlocked its doors as they entered. By this time, both Joel and Priya had become recognizable fixtures in the store, having already purchased the two computers and wireless internet for his home office several days before. It was not hard to forget this mature, white doctor in the company of a young and beautiful Indian woman, especially when they bought so much equipment and paid cash for everything.

"See? This is what I'm talking about, Joel. This—right here." Walking over into the computer games section, Priya pointed to a long, slender box with lights and sensors. This is the Xbox 360 Kinect System. It's a motion sensor, which detects movement and allows you to interface with the game without using a mouse or keyboard." She moved her hands around, trying to get the game to play.

A young man wearing a royal blue Best Buy polo shirt came over to offer his assistance. He remembered Priya and Joel, having seen them there before almost every day that week. "Can I help you?" he asked.

"Yes," Joel answered. "Can you briefly show me how this works?"

"Sure," the young man replied. He proceeded to demonstrate how to work the system in order to play some of the new games, designed to work with the motion sensor. He then encouraged both Joel and Priya to try it out. Joel waved his hands up and down, trying to interact with the demonstration game. He played a game of video Skee-Ball.

"I know that they have been using this technology at MIT and have been modifying it for their own purposes. We could do the same. It connects to USB, and it has voice activation technology incorporated into it. I think we could work with this, Joel."

So Joel gave the order for the young salesman to bring out ten sensors. "Too bad we don't work on commission here," the young man joked. "I would be making a killing off of you guys."

"Fine," stated Joel. "You can just bring them all out front. We're going to go over and buy another twenty desktop computers now."

"And three cameras," added Priya.

"—and three cameras," restated Joel.

"—two wireless remotes..."

"Yes, two wireless remotes..."

"Oh, we'll have to have at least a couple of laser printers, surge protectors, microphones..." Priya recited her mental list.

Joel just looked at the salesman and shrugged.

"Perhaps you should consider having all this stuff delivered, Doctor Russell," the salesman suggested.

"You're quite right," Joel agreed. "Let's make arrangements to do that."

Chapter 13- The Building of Project Séance

It wasn't long before most of the hardware components for the project were purchased, delivered, assembled, and ready for the next stage of development. It had only been a brief period of time since Joel and Priya officially began Project Séance. Priya was amazed at how one with unlimited financial resources could expedite even the seemingly impossible. If a potential seller indicated any hesitancy to provide services on a timely basis, Joel would offer to pad their pockets a bit, and their project would simply move to the top of the contractor's list of priorities. *Yes*, Joel thought, *money can't always buy happiness, but it sure can make a lot of good things happen.*

After the initial month of building preparation, the room construction and reinforcement was complete. The rewiring had also been finished not long after that. And, once the items were delivered, unpackaged, and assembled, it didn't take Priya long to get the computer network up and functional.

Priya was now three months pregnant and visibly showing. She and Joel worked side by side, but she had struggled during this entire trimester with morning sickness. Often, she would work on the project and then stop and run to the rest room to vomit. Still, she maintained an optimistic outlook. Joel tried to encourage her by assuring her that the worst feelings of sickness would most likely subside before long. "The second trimester of pregnancy is usually the easiest," he assured her.

Priya would have preferred the encouragement of a female mentor, who knew firsthand about the strange feelings and moodiness that went along with being a pregnant woman. How she wished her mother would help her through this experience and share these moments with her. She wished she could rely on her mother's valuable advice to prepare her for what lay ahead. True, Joel was a physician. So was her husband, Raminder. But Raminder tended to minimize her discussions about pain, discomfort, or sadness and self-doubt. It wasn't really his fault. He was still only a man.

Joel was a little more sensitive to Priya's pregnancy than Raminder was. Joel's entire career was about dealing with human beings and their emotions. Still— he wasn't a woman—and he didn't know what it was truly like to be pregnant. But he did understand how the undeniably strong feelings of motherhood now consumed Priya. He enjoyed watching her grow as a woman in preparation for motherhood. He was sure she always had a pleasant demeanor, but Joel welcomed her newfound enthusiasm for life—and his project—brought on by the awareness of the new life growing inside of her. He felt working with Priya was good for him. He was sad to consider that—once the project was launched—she would no longer be working alongside him anymore.

Joel thought that it was somewhat ironic that Priya was about to bring new life into this world, yet she was simultaneously immersed in this project with an old man obsessed with communicating with the dead. But Priya's Hindu-based philosophies didn't require that she needed to reconcile this apparent dichotomy of ideals. She justified this project as a means to provide a better future for her family and her child, and this made her happy. Indeed, Joel found her good spirits so infectious that he discovered a renewed zest for life, just being in her company every day.

He knew she would make a great mother. In the past, Joel had always believed that, had Elsa been able to have children, she would have been a marvelous mother. He recalled often watching Elsa as she had volunteered time with various children's charities. When she had the opportunity to interact with them from time to time—meeting with them, reading to them—they seemed to appreciate that she treated them as small adults and didn't seem to treat them the way other grownups treated kids. Because she respected them and didn't threaten them or overpower them with affection, the children loved Elsa. Yes, *everyone* loved Elsa.

Like Priya's pregnancy, the project was divided into trimesters. The initial planning stages took only a few weeks, but Joel and Priya had worked around the clock. The second stage—preparation of the network location and assembly of equipment—was also almost complete. Missing hardware consisted of some special order "ghostbuster equipment" which Priya had ordered express delivery online. The third stage consisted of software design and engineering. This would take much longer and would also require the assistance of quite a few additional freelance programmers whom Priya had outsourced from India. They would need to work 24/7 to get the project finished.

But the fact that the project deadline coincided with Priya's expected delivery date was non-negotiable. It was an all-or-nothing deal. If the project was a failure, there would be no retakes or revisions once the baby was born. It would either be a complete success or a horrible failure. And, at this point in his life, even if it *was* a failure, Joel didn't care. Joel's involvement in this project gave him something to live for and distracted him from constantly reliving the mistakes of his past. In the meantime, Priya's company prevented him from feeling too lonely.

Chapter 14- The Phone Call

Dr. Russell's cell phone rang in the middle of the night, as it charged on the nightstand next to his bed. He had been sleeping soundly but managed to push his hand out in the darkness, grappling for the phone.

What time is it? he asked himself. He checked the display on the phone, which read 12:32 A.M.

Sleepily, Joel picked up the phone and sat upright in his bed. Elsa soundly slept next to him.

"Hello, Doctor Russell? "

"Yes."

"This is Pam Ellis. I am an Intake Specialist in the ER here at St. Johns. Doctor, I hate to disturb you at this time of night, but I have a patient by the name of Jacob Sternen, asking to be admitted to the Behavioral Health Unit. He insists on talking with you."

"He doesn't have to admit himself in order to talk with me. He just needs to call the office in the morning to schedule an appointment. What's the situation?"

"The patient is an ex-Army Sergeant who sustained a traumatic brain injury after a roadside bomb exploded in Afghanistan a year ago. He was honorably discharged, but he states he has recently been diagnosed with Schizophrenia and Post-Traumatic Stress Disorder."

"Why doesn't he seek treatment at the VA Hospital?"

"That's the thing. He insists on seeing and talking to *you*. I tried to explain to him that we really could only admit him in an emergency situation—if he posed an immediate threat to himself or somebody else. Otherwise, he would need to follow up with his psychiatrist at the VA Hospital. But when I told him that, he became angry. He told me again that he had a message for *you*, and that he needed to see *you*. He started cursing obscenities, and stated he didn't want those 'quacks' at the VA anywhere near him."

"He didn't want to cooperate at all?"

"No. When he realized that Doctor Roberts didn't want to admit him unless he posed an immediate threat to himself or others, he threatened a pink lady, who happened to walk by."

"What did he do?"

"He pulled a ball point pen off my desk, grabbed her around the neck from behind, and threatened to stab her with it, if we didn't admit him. I managed to call Security who came to restrain him, eventually talked him out of the pen, and he let the volunteer go. They took him up to the ward to put him in seclusion. Doctor Roberts is the physician on call. He has given orders to sedate Mister Sternen, but the patient insists that he will only talk to *you*."

"How is the Pink Lady? Is she okay?"

"Yes. I apologized to her, and she assured me that she was fine. She wasn't shaken at all. As a matter of fact, Sergeant Sternen also apologized to her as Security hauled him up to the unit."

"So, was he truly threatening her?" Joel inquired.

"Well, Doctor, I can't say. But the Pink Lady didn't think so. Actually, when Mister Sternen apologized to her, she thanked *him*."

"*Thanked* him?"

"Yes. She looked a little flushed, but she said it was the most excitement she had working here all year."

□□□□□□□

Joel's phone rang again. This time, he opened his eyes wider and picked up the phone to see the time on the display. It was 10 P.M. It was not really very late, but he had stayed home tired and sick that entire week and went to bed early that evening.

"Joel? Are you there, Joel? Hello?" It was Priya.

"Yes. Hello, Priya. What's up?"

"I've got something I need to show you in the morning. Can you meet me at the warehouse at 6:30 A.M.?"

"Sure. See you then." Although he thought perhaps he felt awake enough to remember his scheduled meeting with Priya, he was still in a dreamlike state. Confused, he reached over to Elsa's side of the bed to touch her.

Of course, Elsa wasn't there.

Chapter 15- A Renewed Enthusiasm

When Joel reported to the warehouse location at the appointed time, Priya was already busy inside working. She seemed apparently in a happy mood, and he concluded that she had finally overcome her bouts with morning sickness.

"You've got to see this, Joel. These ghosts are going to have a great time! It will be like an arcade for spirits."

There were empty boxes stacked up against the wall. Joel had figured that Priya had recently received a large shipment of items, which she hastily unpacked in her excitement to get things set up. "Some of this is standard paranormal equipment— EMF detectors with USB capabilities and temperature readout, triple-axis gauss meters with PC interfaces and data logging, infrared thermometers, audio amplifiers, ion counters, USB Geiger counters, and the like. So, at least one or more of these are going to be hooked up to a computer, which will record activity on an ongoing basis."

She brought Joel over to look at some large touchscreen monitors they had purchased. "Look at this." Joel looked at what appeared to be a Ouija Board visible on the monitor's display. "This infrared touchscreen detects even the slightest disruption in the LED beam pattern. Watch." She motioned her fingers over the letters of the video Ouija Board, not even touching the screen. Below the Ouija Board display appeared a word processing screen, which printed out her selected letters. "Essentially, this is recording input, so they can chat with people. There are three of these. In the morning, you can review the log and conversations that have occurred. Just click the 'Review History Icon' and scroll up."

"She moved over to another corner of the room. These lights overhead," she pointed upward, "—they shine down on the floor. You know, just like at the Science Center. When you move your feet around, you can manipulate that screen over there and do the exact same thing." She moved quickly now. "Here are a couple more touchscreens with typewriter keyboard interfaces, if you don't want to use the Ouija Board— you know, for the more technologically advanced ghosts who know how to type."

She pointed to the upper corners of the room. "There are camcorders and audio recorders at crucial points around this room, which digitally record all the activity here." Priya started to jump around, almost ecstatic. "These two computers here download every obituary from every newspaper in the country automatically at 5 A.M. That information is incorporated into a database which keeps track of birthdates, death dates, and circumstances of death, if available. I have already downloaded all available death records from social security records and ancestry.com. "

"Priya moved over to a living area on the far side of the third floor space, which she had furnished with several antique chairs of different eras, including several styles of rockers, wing chairs, and carved wooden chairs she had purchased at local antique shops located down the street. "This large screen movie monitor plays movies all day long. You know, old classic epic movies, silent films, documentaries— stuff the spirits might be able to relate to and watch. You know, so they can be entertained." Priya smiled. Joel got a big kick out of watching her talk on about entertaining ghosts. She no longer seemed to be the skeptic he had met before. She talked as though, not only did she believe in ghosts, she actually *believed* that maybe a ghost might enjoy sitting down to a Charlie Chaplin movie in order to escape afterlife boredom.

She pointed out an antique player piano against the far wall, should the ghosts need to entertain themselves with music. If they didn't know how to play, the player portion was fully functional and fairly easy to operate. Stacked on top of the piano was a complete library of rolls of songs popular throughout history. Also, Priya had set up miscellaneous items in this section which she intentionally placed there. Most of them were antiques, but all of them were a sundry assortment of what she perceived might have had a strong sentimental value to someone in the past. These objects might have a significant holographic imprint and special significance for somebody long dead. And both Joel and Priya agreed there might be some plausibility to the theory that certain paranormal activity might not be spirits at all, but just residual energy left behind by people while they lived.

Joel thought it almost comical to watch Priya's excitement for the project. "I went down to the local antique shops and bought some of this other stuff on eBay. That stuff, there on the wall—all old articles and pictures I bought online about the brewery and its history. Over there—a bassinette containing some antique dolls. Toys, here and there. There is an antique desk I found at an auction nearby."

Priya seemed to enjoy this part of the project—the part where she got to spend a lot of cash making a bunch of impulse buys. Things had always been tight for her and Raminder, and they always had to be very careful with their purchases—even the smallest ones. When she went to the antique stores, she could look at items and buy them, just because she liked the way they looked, and because she thought—if *she* liked them, they might have had special meaning to someone in the past.

Joel had been distracted by so much of the surrounding technology before him, he hadn't even noticed the familiar Rococo desk, once belonging to Elsa. When he recognized it, he walked up to it and asked, "Where did you find this?"

"There was an antique auction held nearby. I needed to get out, so I went there the other day with

Raminder. I found this desk, and I thought maybe it had a bit of history behind it. So I bought it. You know, Raminder was freaking out, trying to figure out what the heck I was doing buying such an expensive item. He seemed kind of mad, too. He thought it was a complete waste of money. I told him that you needed a desk for your equipment at home, and you wanted me to buy an antique. I guess he stopped complaining when he figured it was *your* money and *you* could spend it however you wanted to."

Joel ran his hands across the length of familiar desk which had seemed to miraculously find its way back to him. *What a strange coincidence*, he thought.

Chapter 16- Welcome to www.projectseance.com.

Joel sat next to Priya as she handled the layout of the web site they had established for the project. Priya was now five months pregnant, and the project had now officially entered the software development stage. She followed her layout, assembled code, and consulted with Joel next to her. All the while, she fielded numerous calls from developers in India, who had questions about some of the logistics of the software and interface. Only Priya and Joel knew of the exact nature of the project. But she managed to farm most of her development out to programmers in India in small enough bites that they didn't seem to ask a whole lot of nosey questions. As long as the money kept flowing, nobody seemed to care a whole lot about what the two were really trying to achieve.

"So, here is the interface. The user's identity is automatically registered in the database when the death records have been downloaded with his or her information. You can't log on unless you're dead."

"Or pretending to be dead?" Joel asked.

Priya acknowledged his question. "True. That is possible."

"But not likely if we do not advertise the project's existence—" Joel added. "—and knows who is registered in the database and pretends to be that person."

"Yes. That is correct. It is easier to steal a dead person's identity than it is a living person's identity." Priya continued. "So, once the user sets up his account and successfully logs into the sign on screen, he can start to access the network just like any other social networking system out there. He can p—" Priya was suddenly interrupted by a strange sensation.

"What is it?"

She smiled. "It's the baby. I feel him kicking." Priya grabbed Joel's hand and placed his palm on her belly over her loose, cotton tunic. Initially, Joel felt slightly uncomfortable and concerned, because Priya was not overtly physical. Aside from their initial handshake, he had never touched her for fear that she might consider his actions inappropriate.

"Feel it?"

Joel just sat there, feeling a bit uncomfortable. Priya still held his hand on her belly, waiting. Just then, he felt a forceful "whomp" against his palm. "Oh my God!" he cried in amazement, pulling his hand away. "That's incredible! Your kid is going to be a fighter, Priya!"

"I think it will be a boy. At first, I had been feeling little flutters, not knowing what they were. But that is definitely his first, good kick."

"Perhaps he will be a soccer player," Joel joked.

"World Cup, here comes Raminder Junior!" Priya laughed.

He was initially uncomfortable with her taking his hand, but Joel was ultimately glad that Priya shared such an intimate moment with him. And, he was glad for his friend Priya, because she was happy.

After the brief interruption, the two refocused on their work, which was completing Project Séance. But this time, Joel stood behind Priya, listening to her discuss the project plans as she pointed to a spreadsheet she had created on the monitor. She was now four months from her due date, and they still had much to accomplish.

As Joel stood behind her, listening to her talk, he noticed how Priya's long, black hair glistened like silk. He suddenly seemed aware of the smell of her hair—the soothing smell of coconut oil. He daydreamed about lazing on a warm ocean beach somewhere, drinking something with an umbrella in it, without a care in the world.

Now, he no longer paid attention to what Priya said. He simply watched her. He studied her intensity and level of engagement in the project. He noticed her deep, brown complexion, those huge doe eyes, and the way her ruby and vermeil earrings dangled precariously from her tiny ear lobes. She was a beautiful woman, and Joel suddenly felt a bit jealous at the realization that his young colleague Raminder was truly a lucky man. He hoped, for the sake of his young friend, that Dr. Singh would never take his good fortune or his beautiful young wife for granted.

Chapter 17- The Ghostly Sitting Room

Even with the walls now reinforced in the sturdy old building, Joel could still hear the vibrating noise of bands playing on the floor below. Despite the noise, the hour was late. And Joel was too tired to drive the short distance back to his Dogtown rental home. He decided to stay in the sitting room of the laboratory to watch a DVD of *Houdini*, the 1953 movie starring Tony Curtis and Janet Leigh.

For some reason, he wasn't really paying attention to the movie at all. Instead, he thought about Jake Sternen, whom he had managed to forget since his project began. He thought about the man and wondered where on earth he might be.

He recalled his first encounter with Jake at the psychiatric hospital. Knowing what little information he had been given about Jake, Dr. Russell knew about the brain injury Jake sustained while serving during Operation Enduring Freedom in Kandahar in 2002. He had extensively studied the MRIs, CT Scans, and neurological reports provided by the Army hospital. Jake was quite lucky to have survived at all, considering the fact that three fellow soldiers were killed in the same blast, when Jake's unit inadvertently encountered a roadside bomb.

Aside from a small scar above his right eyebrow, Jake bore no other outwardly visible scars of the ordeal. By the time Dr. Russell first met him, Jake had grown his hair out from the conventional buzz cut given to him during his time in the service. Joel figured he had probably put on about thirty to forty pounds since leaving the Army, most likely due to decreased physical activity. Had he not known that Jake enlisted in the Service, he probably would have guessed he was a college dropout or career party animal. He was about twenty-one years old, cleanly shaven, short—maybe 5'6"—and stocky. He was average looking with brown eyes and mousy brown hair.

But Jake possessed a sincere and very expressive face. Joel found that, during the short time he spent with his patient, he could often tell what Jake thought simply by reading these obvious facial expressions. And this was not because Dr. Russell was professionally trained at reading people; it was because Jake *always* wore his feelings on his shirt sleeve. Despite Jake's apparent breaks with reality, he was generally forthright and had a great deal of integrity. And, because Jake was essentially an honest person, Joel had decided early on that he liked him.

Joel understood that Jake was overwhelmed by feelings of guilt that he had managed to survive the attack in Kandahar, when all of his close buddies had been killed. When Joel recalled meeting Jake for the first time after his admission, Jake had insisted upon seeing him. Jake's brain injury not only earned him an honorable discharge, but he was diagnosed with both Paranoid Schizophrenia, as well as having understandably suffered from Post-Traumatic Stress Disorder.

Joel had only a brief discussion with Jake before he realized that he was completely delusional. Jake actually believed that, since the accident, he had the ability to see into the future. In addition, Jake stated that he felt that God had spared his life in Afghanistan, because He wanted him to seek out Dr. Russell to prevent him from committing some horrible future act. Joel confirmed Jake's prior diagnosis and eventually worked toward transferring him to the VA. But Jake was enraged by the fact that Dr. Russell did not believe in his special powers. Consequently, he threatened the doctor's life.

Jake's threat was not the first one Joel ever received from a patient. But Dr. Russell knew that Jake was his only patient who had both the means and the expertise to follow through with such a threat. However, he soon lost track of Jake, once he had been transferred to the VA, mistakenly believing that more competent professionals were caring for him. As a matter of fact, Joel didn't see Jake at all until that night at the parking garage. When he glanced over at Jake through the smoke and fire, Joel could instantly read on his face the look of horror in the discovery that he had killed Dr. Russell's wife instead of killing Dr. Russell, as he originally intended.

Joel felt sorry for Jake. After seven years, he had long forgiven Jake for Elsa's death. He hadn't seen Jake at all since his sentencing, but Joel recalled watching Jake's expression as the judge handed down his sentence. He held his head in shame, gazing down at the floor. It was as if he had been drained of all the fire, energy, and spirit that he once possessed.

Joel felt he and Jake had an unusual connection. They had a great deal in common. In a way, their lives were both spared when others closest to them had been killed. And after this loss, they seemed to simply exist—like walking corpses—trying to find meaning, but unable to forget the past. *Yes,* Joel thought, *Jake and I do have a lot in common.*

Dr. Russell fell asleep in an ornate and very uncomfortable antique chair, very shortly after the movie had begun. For some reason, he was moved by watching Tony Curtis and Janet Leigh's kiss onscreen. He thought of the Hollywood couple, and he noted how the couple's convincingly passionate relationship as Harry and Bess Houdini seemed to be a reflection of Curtis and Leigh's own well-publicized marriage. Joel dreamed of romance, and he wondered if he might ever find his own romance again. Was Elsa the only woman he would ever love during his lifetime? Although he never outwardly admitted to Joanna that he loved her, perhaps he did. Perhaps he should try to rekindle their affair. Or maybe he would find another soulmate. He drifted off to sleep.

"Joel?" Elsa sat at the Rococo writing desk on the far wall, talking to him. She turned around. "Would you sign this sympathy card?" Elsa always sent sympathy cards to family members of departed loved ones. Joel couldn't keep up with the growing list of deceased and affluent Saint Louis socialites and physicians. That was Elsa's job.

Joel seemed preoccupied with a book, but agreed to sign the card for her. She walked it over and handed it to him. "Who's it for?" he asked.

"Me, silly. *I* died." Elsa smiled at him.

"Joel? Joel?" Priya entered the room and turned on the lights. "Did you sleep here all night? That chair is really less for sitting and more for show."

Joel awoke and rubbed his eyes. "I must have." Rising he asked, "What time is it?"

"It is 8 A.M. I know I am late," she apologized. "I haven't been sleeping well lately. My back has been troubling me."

Joel didn't really care that Priya was late. She had put in a lot of long hours in the last few months. But he did notice that she now looked worn. Her belly and breasts had grown huge, and she seemed obviously uncomfortable. He felt sorry for her. He

112

remembered a pregnant patient once telling him that God could make a baby in the blink of an eye. But instead, he gives a woman nine months to think about it. He also remembered the same patient complaining that she had grown so huge in the last trimester, that she wanted "nothing more than to pop the little bastard out". She grew tired of constant backaches, and never being able to see how swollen her ankles had become.

"Perhaps, Priya, we should take what we have and just launch this puppy," Joel suggested. "What more do we have to do?"

"Well, honestly, not much of anything. You know enough about it to maintain it. All the hardware is in place. The system is up. True, there might be a few software bugs, but it's not like a dead person is going to call us up for technical support. Why are you so anxious to start?" Priya asked.

"You look tired, Priya. You need to start focusing on having this baby and on your due date. Instead of buying this crap, you need to buy a crib and baby clothes and diapers, and whatever the hell kind of baby junk you buy for new babies. You need to move on with your life. All I really have to do is....just flip the switch and sit back and wait for something to happen." Joel stretched out his hands and smiled.

When Project Séance finally did go live, nothing memorable happened, but everything worked as expected. Instruments hummed along, cameras scanned and homed, and everything seemed to come together seamlessly and uneventfully. Soon, their final workday together had ended, and Joel and Priya headed out the front door.

"Don't you think—now that I will no longer be here—you should share the access code with someone else—you know, just in case something happens?"

"Who would I share it with? The ghosts?" Joel laughed. "Ghosts don't need a key."

From that point forward, Joel tried to resume his former, empty life and tend to the normal activities of daily living. Typically, he would rise late in the morning and report to the warehouse about mid-afternoon. He would perform his daily maintenance, which usually took about an hour tops. His tasks included archiving recently downloaded data, reviewing audio and video recordings for any anomalies, resetting tapes and reviewing activity logs, and rebooting computers weekly. At first, he would recline in one of the massive antique chairs and select old movies to watch. Then he subscribed to local cable stations and just kept the TV running when he went home at night. *Maybe the spirits care about current events,* he would absurdly comment to himself.

When Joel reviewed the data logs, he did note anomalies occurring throughout the room. They were apparent on the infrared, temperature, and EMF detectors, as well as heightened radioactivity registering on the Geiger counters. This activity usually peaked when Joel was not present, but even when he was in the room, was still there. Unfortunately, Joel didn't notice or sense anything extraordinary during these times. He thought that perhaps he needed to hire Ariel to come up there and hang out. Maybe she would be able to sense something he couldn't—something strangely metaphysical.

Occasionally, when Joel fell asleep in the sitting room, he would experience some very odd and vivid dreams. Often, he dreamed of Elsa. Sometimes, he would dream of someone else who had died—usually someone he had known previously. But Joel was ultimately starting to believe that his entire project was a failure. It was naïve to think that ghosts, or spirits, or whatever the hell they were—actually existed. And it was crazy to think that, if they did exist, they would have any interest at all in communicating with the living. Maybe, if spirits really did exist, they simply wanted what he wanted—to be left alone.

Nevertheless, Joel regarded the project space as a kind of refuge, even if it was an experimental failure. He would spend time whiling away the hours reading history books, watching TV, and playing the old player piano Priya had purchased. Several keys were broken, and the piano was sorely out of tune. But for a neglected antique, it really wasn't a bad instrument.

One day Joel was playing his rendition of *Caravan*, a former Duke Ellington song he had taught himself as a teenager. The piano cover suddenly slammed down heavily on his knuckles, bruising his hands. Fortunately, nothing was broken. While Joel tried to explain it away by blaming himself for pounding a little too heavily on the keyboard, he never attempted to play that song again.

Often, when he returned to the project, Joel would notice other objects had been moved or relocated. But Joel was pushing fifty-six, and it wasn't uncommon for him to move and misplace things. He lost track of his cell phone and his keys constantly and even forgot the names of people and places he had known for years. If something was out of place, it was probably because *he* had misplaced it.

Soon it was October. This was a busy time at the brewery and mansion due to the many haunted cave tours being held there for Halloween, and parking became problematic for the regular renters at the brewery. Joel showed up less frequently during this time to avoid the dilemma of having to find a parking space close by. Sometimes he would get a cab. But finding a cab to drive him home was a little tougher than getting one to bring him there.

Joel grew bored with his failed project and had become utterly disappointed that it was nothing more than a very expensive flop. A few times, during his hallway tours to the bathroom, he occasionally passed Ariel. But she was usually busy practicing and had very little time to strike up conversations. On the other hand, Bruce, the bass player in Ariel's band, loitered about quite regularly. Joel wasn't even sure he had a home. He seemed very friendly, but he tended to follow Joel around a little too much at times and sometimes cramped his style.

So, overcome with boredom at the brew house, and believing there wasn't a "flying frig" going on with his disastrous experiment, Joel gave up on Project Séance. Instead, he decided that he would have to venture out and discover life.

Chapter 18- The Baby Shower

"Joel! I have a son!"

That was the complete message Raminder left on Joel's voice mail. During the last few weeks prior to her due date, Priya was not feeling well at all. Finally, she delivered a fine, healthy son two weeks early. Joel sensed the sheer excitement in Raminder's voice, even though the message was brief.

When the baby was one month old, the happy young couple invited Joel and a few close friends and associates to a celebratory dinner and baby shower at a local Indian restaurant. Raminder still beamed from the excitement of becoming a new father. He greeted Joel outside the restaurant, after Joel parked his car, and he handed him a cigar. He put his arm around Joel's back and escorted him into the building. Even from the street corner, Joel could smell the strong spices wafting out into the street. Placing the still wrapped cigar in his mouth and modeling a W.C. Fields stance, Joel joked. "Well, you gotta do this right."

"I am very happy, my friend. And we have you to thank for much of this." Raminder told him. "Priya and I have been very lucky that you needed her for this project." Raminder stopped Joel at the entrance, facing him. "Look, Joel. I know that you were just looking for a way to help us out by keeping her busy, and I appreciate that." He nodded his head, chuckled, and then walked Joel into the front door. "Project Séance, indeed!"

Raminder knew all along what Joel and Priya were up to. Joel figured that Raminder perceived the project as an empty diversion for Priya. He may have even seen it as nothing more than a very expensive joke. But, thanks to Joel's generosity, Raminder and Priya were now completely out of debt. They had brilliant futures ahead of them and a strong, healthy son.

Joel had not had Indian food in a long time. The rich smells he encountered inside brought his olfactory senses to life. The food was exquisite, and the company was friendly. Priya sat at a table, holding her young son proudly. The child was very small, but he looked very much like a miniature Raminder. Raminder stood next to his wife for most of the evening beaming—that is, when he wasn't bragging to the guests and handing out cigars. The ladies in attendance approached the baby, trying to catch a glimpse of his angelic face. They would coo and smile if they thought the baby was responding to them. "He likes me!" a few would brag.

Raminder insisted that his good friend sit next to him at the party. Small bowls of *kheer*, a popular rice pudding dish, were being served for dessert. Raminder pushed a bowl over to Joel. "Eat up, my friend. The milk will help counteract the spices. This is comfort food. You know—rice is to Asians what potatoes are to white people!"

Even though Joel knew nobody at the party but Priya and Raminder, he felt happy in the company of friends. He had spent much of his recent life alone, and he had decided he enjoyed this feeling of being needed—the feeling that he belonged.

Chapter 19- Doctor Russell's New Job

Joel had decided to volunteer his services with the Missouri Department of Mental Health, working with troubled teens in Saint Louis, who had been referred by Family Court. Well, it wasn't exactly volunteer work, because he received a small stipend for his expertise and services. But he considered it volunteer work nonetheless. Money didn't motivate him to accept the job. He had plenty of money, and he didn't really care what the job paid.

He felt that dealing with troubled teens would be a good way of getting back into practice, relying on his expertise, yet still permitting him to remain fairly undetached. He felt that this demographic might be good to work with, because some of these kids still had a promising life ahead. They just needed a good kick in the right direction in order to turn their lives around. Perhaps he could help motivate them to make a difference.

Dr. Russell would consult with outpatient teens referred to his facility and those in the inpatient setting. These were kids who had anger management issues, substance abuse problems, and family crisis issues. His work proved very frustrating most of the time, because he often felt that he really had no impact on these kids' lives and the stupid choices they made. Many were uncooperative and noncompliant. When he did have the opportunity to meet their troubled parents—if they had parents—he understood the roots of the old adage that "the apple really doesn't fall far from the tree". At times, he would be so unspeakably frustrated with the system, the kids, and the parents, that he sometimes wished for his days practicing psychiatry in Chesterfield, where it seemed as though those problems really didn't seem like real problems at all. But he kept all these thoughts to himself, never admitting them to anyone.

Shortly after beginning his work at the center, Joel met an intriguing girl, named Tunisha Wallis. She was a young runaway—an African-American girl of fifteen. She stood about 5'4", but even for a young girl of fifteen, was very developed for most girls her age. She had very generous hips and a small waist. Like all girls her age, she was sometimes self-conscious about her weight. Her face was friendly and sincere. Her lips were full, her nose was wide, and her eyes were a deep brown. She kept her hair in a medium length bob, simple and straightened. She had a friendly personality and strived to please everyone most of the time, but she seldom smiled. On rare occasions, Joel would feel privileged and pleased when she did allow him to catch a glimpse of her smile. And when she did smile, he felt overcome by a tremendous sense of warmth and goodness.

Fortunately, Tunisha hadn't been on the streets long before the State placed her as a resident in the center. She lagged several years behind in her academics, but the teaching staff there noted that she was "smart as a whip", catching up quickly, and even surpassing many of her peers with her zest for learning. She had been a resident at the facility for several months before Joel met her, and she immediately struck Dr. Russell as an inspiring young woman. When he felt bogged down in work or self-doubt, he would welcome the opportunity to talk to her.

They initially hit it off well. Soon she opened up about her past and recounted some of the horrors she had experienced during her lifetime, and Joel soon realized how strong this girl was to have the drive to turn her life around, despite a childhood plagued with trauma.

Tunisha's father had left her mother when she was little, and she had been sexually abused by her mother's live-in boyfriend. She had been bounced from foster home to foster home from ages twelve to fifteen, when she finally ran off to live in the streets. There she would beg or, if necessary, turn tricks for food or drugs. He recalled meeting her in his office for the first time, along with her foster mother. The two were seated in front of Joel's desk. Tunisha's foster mother was busily adjusting the large amounts of visible cleavage in the young girl's blouse.

"You gotta be a little more modest, baby." She pulled up at the neckline of Tunisha's wardrobe. "Leave somethin' for the imagination!"

Joel was amused. As he talked with Tunisha and her foster mother, he became aware that Tunisha's foster mother really cared about her and tried very hard to be a good role model. She worked as a cook in a local elementary school cafeteria and had several other foster children in her care.

Joel directed his question at Tunisha. "Tunisha, why did you decide to run away?"

Tunisha didn't answer, so her foster mother answered for her. "She don't like rules, Doctor. We were makin' her go to church and do chores. You know, things good girls are supposed to do. We been tryin' to adopt her."

"Is that true, Tunisha?"

"Yeah, Doctor Joel. But my real momma don't want nothin' to do with it. You know, I think she don't want me to be happy."

Tunisha's foster mother chimed in again. "I told her. Baby, I don't care! I want you anyway. You can stay with me for as long as you like. You just gotta follow rules and go to church." Tunisha's foster mother looked at Joel earnestly. "You see, Doctor. Tunisha's been hurt all her life by people she loved. She don't wanna get close to people. She don't wanna get hurt again. And when she does get hurt—well, she kind of expects it. 'Cause that's what she's known all her life. I think that's why she done run away in the first place."

"I see," Joel responded thoughtfully.

During later conversations with Tunisha, Joel learned more about her. She talked about her brief life on the street. She would joke with Joel about his ignorance of all things urban. She often felt it her duty to educate him regarding street slang and the latest rap and hip-hop artists on the charts. Her celebrity role models were Beyoncé and Jennifer Hudson. Of course, Joel was an old man, and he had no real desire to learn about hip-hop culture. But it amused him that Tunisha was so engaged, and if he needed to study up on all things current to get to know her better, then *that* was what he would have to do. She would talk about celebrities and other teens at the center, along with other friends she had made during her stays with various foster parents.

When she entered the center, Tunisha had only briefly experimented with a few drugs. Joel prescribed an antidepressant, but she had not developed any chemical dependencies which required treatment. Medically, she was in good health, but she did manage to contract *Trichomonas* and *Chlamydia*, two sexually transmitted diseases, during her time out on the streets.

Tunisha joked about having "itchy cootchie" and "a lady box that smelled like catfish", when describing her symptoms. She also mentioned a girlfriend who was going to have a baby and wanted to name it "Chlamydia", because she liked the way the name sounded.

Joel laughed. "What did you tell her?"

"I told her she was stupid! I said, 'Don't you know what that means?' She was so dumb!"

"So, did she name the baby Chlamydia?"

"No, thank God! She named it India. That sounded like a much better name," Tunisha answered.

"Yes," Joel agreed. "—much better. But you were fortunate, Tunisha."

"What do you mean, Doctor Joel?"

"Well, when you were out on the streets having unprotected sex, you could have contracted something much worse than an STD. You could have gotten pregnant, contracted AIDs, or even gotten killed," Joel commented.

"You're right, Doctor Joel. I don't need no baby right now," Tunisha agreed.

"You're practically a baby yourself. You need to work on getting your life back in order. We're going to help you try and do that," Joel assured her.

At times, Tunisha would still grapple with moods of depression and consider ending it all. Due to disruptions in her education, her language skills were lacking, and she did suffer from a learning disability. But she would often write poetry and lyrics in several journals she kept with her. When she could, she would spend time in the small library at the school, studying and working on the computer. Dr. Russell and the other staff members encouraged this practice, because it was both a therapeutic outlet and a great means of creative expression.

Tunisha had made friends easily at the center. But she did have one love interest—another young man there—who was the same age as she was. Joel was puzzled as to what she saw in the boy. The young man's name was Antony, and although he left the center one month before Joel joined the staff, Joel's colleagues had filled him in on his history and character. Like Tunisha, Antony also had a history of drug addiction and childhood abuse. But he often exhibited violent behavior, and he didn't seem very interested in her. During the few times that he did choose to interact with her, he was often abusive toward her, calling her names and belittling her about her weight.

After Antony had been released from the center back into his grandmother's care, he became involved in a gang in North Saint Louis. Late one night, he was involved in a gang war and suffered multiple stab wounds. An ambulance brought him to SSM DePaul Health Center's ER, where he was pronounced dead on arrival.

Tunisha had confided in Joel that she was convinced that Tony truly loved her, but that he never let on, because he thought his friends would make fun of him. She stated that he had actually called her "bootylicious" and that he preferred her ample derrière. Then, on a day when Tunisha seemed especially depressed and confused, she said, "Doctor

Joel, he's sorry for being mean to me, and he wants me to come be with him."

"What makes you think that?" Joel inquired.

"I just know these things, Doctor Joel. I just know."

Chapter 20- The Email from Marta

"What the fuck, Joel? Is this some sort of sick, twisted Halloween joke?"

It *was* Halloween. Joel had checked his morning voice mail messages and heard this one. He recognized it as Joanna's voice, and he replayed it several times. He was sure it was her voice. And she was undoubtedly upset at him. But he hadn't a clue as to what he had done to get her so mad.

He had never known her to be so upset. He called her cell, but she didn't answer her phone. His calls were going straight to voice mail. So, Joel called the office. Ariel answered, and Joel asked if Joanna was there.

"Yeah, but she's holed up in her office and has cancelled all her appointments for the day."

"Do you know what happened?"

"No, but somebody sure pissed her off. She is livid."

"Tell her I'm coming over."

When Joel arrived at the old office, he plowed right past Ariel toward Joanna's closed office door.

Ariel called to him. "She says she doesn't want to talk to you, Joel!"

Joel pounded on Joanna's door. "Open up, Joanna!"

Joanna did not respond. "Open up, Joanna, or I'll break down the door!"

Reluctantly, she opened the door, but first hesitated to let him in. She was mad. But it was more like she had been both *crying mad* and shaking.

"What the hell is going on?" he asked.

"Seriously? So, you want to play dumb now? Look, Joel. I've had it with all your bullshit! You have been playing me since I met you. Isn't it enough that I can never be happy—or in love—because of you?" She harshly glared at him. "I mean, really Joel, isn't it enough you stab me in the heart—now you've got to keep twisting the knife?"

He had never seen her this mad. It didn't seem like the Joanna who seemed obsessed with maintaining her professional appearance at all times. She was screaming at him, and he knew that everyone in the office could hear. Yet today, she was in such a state, she didn't care what everyone else thought of her. She began crying, hysterically.

"Shh...shh...." Joel tried to silence her. "You have *got* to calm down. Tell me—what the hell is going on?"

She just glared at Joel through her tears. Then, she stopped in disbelief. "You mean....you truly don't know?"

"No, I don't. Why are you so upset?"

"Really.....you didn't send that message?"

"I haven't sent anything. What message?"

"That email."

"Not me. Who's it from? What does it say?"

Joanna thought for a moment. She motioned Joel around to the laptop sitting on her desk. She opened her email inbox. "Somebody sent me this message, claiming to be Marta Kennison."

"Marta?"

"Yes." She read the email aloud.

"Hello, Joanna,

Greetings from beyond.

I suppose, by now, you've figured out that my last call was about more than just a seating chart. The issue was really about my youngest daughter moving away to marry and leaving me all alone. I don't do alone very well.

I wish I could have been more straightforward about the whole affair, but we Kennisons aren't very good about discussing our feelings. Don't fret. It's not your fault.

By the way, it's just lovely here. You should visit sometime.

Warmest regards,

Marta"

Marta Kennison was the first of Joanna's patients to commit suicide. After nearly ten years, Joanna had still not overcome her tremendous feelings of guilt over Marta's death. She had always believed that she could have done more to save her.

"What the...." Joel tried to process the email she had just read.

"You mean, you really didn't know about this?"

"I swear. I did *not* send this. Who else knew about Marta?"

"That's just it—no one. Just you, me, and—God rest her soul—Marta."

"You mean you never talked to anyone else about her call about the seating arrangement?"

"No. Seriously, Joel. It wasn't you? If it was, it is a very cruel joke."

"I swear, Joanna. Have I ever tried to hurt you?" Joel asked.

"Only once. But still, I think I *do* believe you."

"Where is it from? What's the email address?"

"Looks like Marta_Kennison06152002@projectseance.com."

Joel was dumbstruck. He recognized the email address as coming from his project website. Priya had set up the system to automatically download death records and user accounts based on the person's first name, underscore, last name, and eight digit date of death.

Joanna noticed Joel's expression had frozen. "What? What's wrong?"

The project! He had completely forgotten about the project! He had abandoned it, because he thought it was a flop. In his haste to start practicing psychiatry again, he had spent the entire month getting familiar with his new patients at the youth center. The last time he reported to the brewery was over three weeks ago.

Joel didn't say anything to Joanna. He left the office in a state of panic. He ran out to Ariel at the front desk and looked at her.

"Keys!"

"What?"

"Do you have your key to the brewery?"

"Huh?"

"I don't have my keys, and I need to go there *now*. Can I borrow yours?"

Ariel fumbled through her purse, and then detached the brewery key from her key ring to give to Joel. He didn't thank her. He simply bolted out of the office to his car and sped away.

Joel screeched up to the old brewery warehouse and hastily parked his car on Cherokee Street. He unlocked the door and ran up the first flight of stairs. Bruce stood at the top of the second floor stairwell and accosted Joel. He was smoking a joint.

"Dude, I know we all get pretty loud here, but what's with that fucking dance team goin' at it at 3 A.M.?"

"What?"

"I'm telling you—they're pretty noisy, even for all the noise that goes on in this place."

"What? Dancing?" Joel seemed a little distracted.

"You know—stomping noises? Dude, it never lets up. It's been going on for weeks. And your band equipment is sucking all the power from this entire building."

Joel ran up the next flight of stairs as Bruce followed. He punched in the security code to the massive door and quickly pushed it open. Bruce stood behind him, and, as his jaw dropped, so too did his joint.

"Awesome, dude! That is one kick-ass light show!"

Dr. Russell couldn't believe what he was seeing. There was a flurry of activity throughout the laboratory. Everything was happening, moving, and blinking, but *nobody* was actually *there*. Joel and Bruce stood at the door, amazed. The two men just stood there, for what seemed like five minutes, just staring into the room and trying to process what was apparently happening inside.

Then, Bruce abruptly bent down, picked up his joint, and ran back down the stairs screaming, "Fuckin' awesome, man! Hey, come look at this shit!"

The project was buzzing. Everything was buzzing. In the sitting room, the two rocking chairs were rocking—as if someone was sitting in them. The piano keyboard would tinkle out a few notes from time to time. Upon close examination, Joel noticed that the roll of music loaded onto the player had been played completely through and needed rewinding. The television was on, but the stations would spontaneously change after every few seconds. The volume would rise to a deafening loudness and then decrease to the point where it was inaudible. Books laid open on the Rococo desk were magically flipping page to page, as if someone sat there, reading.

Past the sitting room, Joel noticed the cameras following him. And, as he approached the computer monitors, he could see that each monitor was being touched. It was extraordinary. It was exciting. He could read the text below the Ouija Board screen where a ghost-user seemed to be typing. It said, *Tell Marilyn to turn off the oven. I left it on when I stuck my head in it.*

Joel scrolled upward. There were all kinds of messages being recorded from a variety of operators. Most of these messages had no meaning for him, but he was sure they did for the poor saps who were typing them. And each computer had days and days' worth of these cryptic messages, which the ghosts had typed in to be read. Joel knew he needed to read through each of these files at some point, and he wondered who the hell these people were.

The Kinect sensors were blinking and moving up and down, and their associated computers were responding to the detected movement throughout the room. But Joel saw no apparitions—only the evidence that something or someone unseen seemed to be lurking there. *Maybe,* he thought, *they weren't really trying to communicate. Maybe they were just trying to entertain themselves.*

Joel walked over to the main console and checked the user database to see who had logged in. There had been 263 users who had added email accounts in the past 24 hours. There were voice recordings and video recordings dating back two and a half weeks ago, which he would need to review. Perhaps he would see an apparition or a spirit, or hear its voice on the recordings. Joel still really didn't know what was really happening, but he did know this about Project Séance: It wasn't a failure at all. He didn't know what the hell it *was*, but it definitely *wasn't* a failure.

Chapter 21- A Terrible Waste

"Doctor Russell," said a voice on the other end of the line, "this is Maggie Johnson, social worker from the center. I'm sorry to call you this early in the morning."

"Sure. What's up, Maggie?"

"I'm afraid I have some bad news for you. Your patient, Tunisha Wallis, tried to commit suicide."

Joel was silent.

"Doctor Russell? Are you there?"

"Yes, I'm here."

"It seems she smuggled a razor blade into her bathroom and damaged her radial artery. Her roommate found her barely alive. We rushed her to the hospital, and they managed to repair the artery and gave her four units of blood. She's very lucky. I'm sorry to have to tell you this, Doctor Russell. The police are here at the center, and they want to talk to you."

"Me, too. I'm sorry, too. I will be there shortly."

When Joel showed up at the center, there were two police officers investigating the staff. They interviewed Joel, also. Unfortunately, the social workers and teachers on staff were probably more helpful answering questions, because Joel had only known Tunisha for a little over a month. He answered their questions as best he could.

He verified what the other staff members had told them, explaining that Tunisha was abused as a child. Despite all the troubles she encountered during her childhood, in successive foster homes, and out in the streets, she was highly intelligent. She seemed to be turning her life around at the center and had a great deal of promise. He admitted that she had bouts of suicidality, but most of the time she seemed to do quite well. Everyone loved her, and she had a marvelous personality. She was fortunate to have survived, because it would have been a tremendous loss if she had not.

The interviewers seemed satisfied with Dr. Russell's statements. After they had interviewed every relevant staff member, they left, believing they had gotten a sufficient amount of information to make a report.

But Joel realized one important thing: he really didn't know Tunisha as well as he thought he did.

After the police investigators left the center, Dr. Russell visited the room that Tunisha Wallis had called her home for the past several months. He made his way through caution tape, which blocked the door. By this time, the police investigators and healthcare professionals had done all that they could do, and they left the room temporarily uninhabited.

He walked over to Tunisha's bed, which was still neatly made, and picked up her teddy bear. No doubt, it had special meaning to her. *I'm sure it has a cute name, too,* he thought. *What a terrible waste.*

He opened the door to the bathroom, where Tunisha's roommate found her unconscious. Tunisha had been taken to the hospital, but a large pool of blood still remained on the floor. Smears of blood and bloody footprints coated the walls and floor. Judging from that bloody mess left behind, he imagined that pure chaos ensued, once she was discovered and efforts were made to save her. Joel felt sick.

"You know, she say he talked to her."

A thin, young, African-American girl with braids, stood at the door. "She say he dead, and he done talked to her."

Joel didn't know the young girl's name, but he deduced that she was probably Tunisha's roommate. She walked in to pick up some personal items from her side of the room. A social worker followed.

"Who talked to her?" Joel asked.

"Dat Tony dude. She say he done talked to her, even tho' he dead. I tol' her—Girl, you crazy! Ain't nobody kin talk to you when he dead! She done lost it. She be writin' in those books all the time." She pointed to Tunisha's journals on her nightstand. "Writin', writin' writin'......She say he want her to come be wit' him. I tol' her—Girl, ain't no man worth dyin' for!"

Joel picked up Tunisha's journals, the notebooks, and teddy bear and took them with him.

Chapter 22- At the Hospital

Tunisha Wallis was admitted to the adolescent psychiatric unit of SSM DePaul Health Center, after unsuccessfully attempting to kill herself. She managed to cut into the radial artery of her left wrist with a razor blade and had lost a great deal of blood. When her roommate discovered her and alerted the staff, she was rushed to the ER, where surgeons successfully repaired the artery. She was given several units of packed red blood cells.

Joel entered Tunisha's room. She lay in the hospital bed, extremely weakened by excessive blood loss. Her right arm was hooked to an IV unit, and her left wrist was thickly bandaged. In the corner of the room stood a very tall, bald, well-dressed black man. He had removed his hat and placed it at his heart and seemed to be watching guard over Tunisha from the darkness.

"Hey, Doctor Joel," Tunisha said weakly.

"Hey there, kiddo. How are you doing?"

"Tired....I guess I did a bad thing, huh?"

"It would have been bad if we'd have lost you. We almost lost you. But you're still here.....That's very good, Tunisha. Very good. Here. Look who came to see you." He handed Tunisha her worn teddy bear.

"Pendergrass," she whispered. Joel could see tears in Tunisha's eyes. "I'm sorry, Doctor Joel," was all she managed to say.

He patted her hand. "You just rest. We'll talk later. You just get better, and we'll talk soon."

"Okay." Tunisha closed her eyes to rest.

Joel turned to the man in the corner, who whispered as he introduced himself. "I'm Pastor Jackson, a friend of Tunisha's foster parents. I came by to visit her."

Pastor Jackson stood before him in a nicely tailored, gray business suit and red checkered necktie. He still held his black trilby hat in his right hand. Standing before him, Dr. Russell—already a tall man—noted that the pastor still stood several inches taller than he. He was built like a football player, but he had a very calm and pensive demeanor, which Joel surmised probably suited him well to his chosen career. The pastor's head was completely bald, but he sported a well-trimmed goatee. He held his brow in an engaged and concerned expression, while he conversed with Joel.

Dr. Russell shook his hand. "Nice to meet you, Pastor. I'm Joel Russell, Tunisha's new psychiatrist at the center."

"Nice to meet you, Doctor. Would you like to step out into the hallway and give her some rest?" The Pastor pointed the way.

"Sure," Joel agreed.

As they stepped out into the hallway, the Pastor looked even more concerned. "Doctor Russell, I am worried that Tunisha is delusional. I think she has started to lose her grip on reality. I mean, she truly thinks this dead young man is trying to talk to her. I believe she believes he is trying to convince her to kill herself."

"You know about this?"

"Why, yes. Her friends and foster mother were concerned about her. Apparently she has hinted about it more than once."

"Well, I haven't been treating her for long, but yes, she has hinted about it. Honestly, It took me by surprise. Recently, she didn't indicate to me she had a serious plan for suicide." Joel paused. "I have her journals. I need to read them and talk to her about it when she is feeling up to it."

"Let me know if there is anything I can do. I am pastor of the Central Seventh Day Adventist Church on Skinker."

"Thank you, Pastor. I will call you."

Chapter 22- Tunisha's Journals

Joel had spent the night awake on his living room sofa in his Dogtown house. He was troubled about the recent events of the day and couldn't sleep. He decided he would read Tunisha's journals and perhaps gain a little more insight into what had prompted her to try and take her own life. And while he read, he realized there was much, much more to Tunisha than she let on.

"My wild and crazy days are gone
There's nothing for me now
I ain't yet fully growed, but yet
I have a wrinkly brow.

And no one understands me
Or the heart ache that I see
Nobody but my Pendergrass
—Just Pendergrass and me.

Teddy Pendergrass. That was the name of her bear. As he read, it broke his heart. What a complete waste, he kept thinking. Such a young girl, with so much life ahead of her.

As he read Tunisha's poetry, he felt overwhelming sadness, thinking of this young life almost lost to suicide. What could he possibly do to save her? Maybe he could have met her earlier and prevented this. He read on. He read poems of despair, love, betrayal, and life out on the streets. Joel realized, on the outside, she seemed happy and glad to be alive. She yearned for acceptance and approval. She would do anything to be loved and cared for. And yet, she was intensely private with her feelings. She had been damaged and ignored, but she was resilient and mature beyond her years.

Then, Joel picked up Tunisha's journal. It began when she had come to live at the center. She had documented everything from her first day there onward. She wrote about the meals, her teachers, her social workers, her roommate, and the young man, Antony, whom she had met and become infatuated with. She even talked about meeting "Doctor Joel," as she called him. How he was an "old man with a kind face." She said she liked him and trusted him.

But Joel was disturbed to study the entries she had written just before her suicide attempt. Her handwriting grew more impulsive, as she wrote about Tony's death. She did believe that Tony had tried to talk to her, and she claimed to be corresponding with him. She believed that Tony wanted her to be with him, dead, like he was. Joel thought as he read, she *was* delusional. Her roommate was right. Pastor Jackson was right. How could he not have seen it?

When Joel turned the page, a loose sheet of paper fell out. He picked the sheet up to read it. It looked like a printed copy of an email addressed to Tunisha. Dr. Russell's heart stopped, and he shook as he read it.

Dear Tunisha,

I am sorry that I was bad to you. I was trying to be cool you know? You know my peeps made fun of me if they think that I liked you. I so sorry I made fun of you. You are not fat, you so fine. You very fine.

I miss you baby. I want you to come be with me. You gotta give me that. I love you Tunisha. Come be with me.

The email was sent from Antony_Johnson09102011@projectseance.com.

Tunisha's roommate was not making all this up. Tunisha was *not* delusional. Antony was sending her this email. And it was coming from Joel's project!

Joel felt sick. Although his experiment had been borne out of his dream to eventually communicate with Elsa and find closure in his own life, he now realized that this Project Séance had become much more than that. Whatever it was, or whoever it was using the system was accomplishing nothing more than to torment the living. In Tunisha's case, someone was out there—maybe it was Tony. But maybe it was some evil spirit or demon or whatever the hell it was—trying to convince her that she was better off dead than alive.

Dr. Russell had to do something about this. He just didn't know what.

Services at the Central Seventh Day Adventist Church on Skinker Boulevard were held each Saturday at 11 A.M. The church, located just south of the Washington University main campus, had many members attending. The congregation was ethnically diverse, but most were residents living east of the inner belt in Saint Louis.

Pastor Jackson preached a sermon on—of all things—the state of the dead. Joel was truly engaged. Having not slept in two days, not only was he surprisingly awake, he was intrigued to hear this pastor's philosophies on what happens to people when they die.

Contrary to many other Protestant and Catholic philosophies, Joel learned, Adventists believe that the dead know nothing. Pastor Jackson quoted the biblical text of Ecclesiastes 9:5, which states, "*The living know that they will die, but the dead know not anything, nor have they any longer a reward, for their memory is forgotten.*"

This made Joel wonder. If this pastor was right about the dead knowing nothing, then what was powering Project Séance? Was it more occult, more evil?

147

After the service, Joel greeted the Pastor, who stood at the exit, bidding goodbye to the congregation.

"Nice to see you again, Doctor Russell."

"Likewise, Pastor Jackson. I enjoyed your sermon."

The pastor laughed. "Yes, I'm a real 'fire and brimstone' kind of preacher. That sells pretty big in this church. Tell me, Doctor, would you care to join us for fellowship dinner?"

Joel really didn't have any place to go for lunch. At home, he may have had a bottle of spoiled milk in the fridge or some moldy bread in the cupboard. So he accepted the invitation. He sat at Pastor Jackson's table partaking in a modest, vegetarian potluck dinner. Joel was not a vegetarian, but he had hardly eaten at all in the last couple of days, and he would have eaten just about anything—vegetable or animal. Surprisingly, most of the food he had selected seemed a little bland, but still somewhat tasty. But Joel was still troubled, and he had a tendency to eat very little when his mind was heavy about things.

Joel decided he would strike up a conversation with the Pastor about his philosophies on the state of the dead.

"Can I ask you something, Pastor?" Joel asked.

Pastor Jackson laughed. "*You* ask *me* something? That's a hoot! Sure, shoot."

"You really don't believe in spirits? You're saying that when we're dead, we're just—"

"—Dead? Pretty much. I believe the dead are just sleeping, waiting for to be resurrected at the Second Coming of Christ." The Pastor turned to Joel and paused. "What is this really about, Doctor Russell? What are you digging for?"

"Well, it's about Tunisha. But it's also about me. But I am trying to decide how to say it. You know, so it doesn't sound completely crazy."

The pastor laughed and cried sarcastically, "Ha! A crazy psychiatrist. Haven't seen one of those—ever!"

Joel laughed. "Well, I have reason to believe someone contacted her, claiming to be this young man and trying to get her to join him in death."

"You know this for a fact?" The Pastor expressed concern. "Tell me what you know."

"I don't think you're going to believe me, if I tell you what I'm about to tell you." Joel warned.

"Well, now, Doctor—you have my undivided attention...."

So Joel proceeded to confess everything. First, he recounted his conversations with Tunisha and her roommate. Then he told the pastor about confiscating and reviewing her journals. When he found the letter, he talked about Project Séance. How he launched it thinking he might be able to talk to spirits. How he thought he might be able to contact his dead wife, Elsa.

"Would you mind my asking you about your wife, Doctor Russell? How did she die?" Pastor Jackson asked.

"She was killed seven years ago in an explosion, set off by a patient of mine," Joel answered.

"A patient?" Pastor Jackson inquired.

"Yes. This patient was an ex-Army Sergeant who suffered a traumatic brain injury when he encountered a roadside bomb in Afghanistan. The bomb he set was intended for me, because this patient claimed that, ever since the explosion, he could see into the future. He said that God had talked to him."

"And did you believe him?"

"Well, no—not initially. I'm a psychiatrist, trained as a scientist. I have dealt with plenty of people who have had breaks with reality and claim to have been spoken to by God. I chalked his visions up as all part of his elaborate delusion." Joel explained his point of view to the pastor almost apologetically.

"You know, Doctor—" The pastor looked solemn.

"—Call me Joel, please."

"—Joel. This makes me think of the story of a woman who was considered one of the founders of our church. Her name was Ellen White." The pastor explained. "Our church is a fairly young one, having been established after the Great Disappointment of 1844. It seems this guy named William Miller claimed that in 1844, Jesus was going to make his Second Coming. So, all these people started selling all their belongings in preparation of the big event. Anyway, the day came and went. Ellen's family was a bunch of Millerites, who reread the prophecies of Daniel and the Revelation to figure out what the heck happened.

"Anyway, this particular woman was struck in the head by a rock when she was a young girl. From that point forward in her life, she claimed to have visions from God where she was able to see into the future. She and her husband helped establish this denomination. She wrote volumes and volumes of religious books, along with counsels on church, family, and education. She claimed that these were all given to her by God. Many in the church today still consider her to be a modern-day prophet.

"What did she prophesy?" Joel seemed fascinated. He had never really known much about Seventh-Day Adventists.

"She predicted occurrences such as the Great San Francisco earthquake of 1906. She made many unpopular statements in her time about the lethality of smoking and alcohol long before these statements were accepted by science. Some say she even saw a vision of 9/11."

Joel sat silent.

Pastor Jackson continued. "I know you were trained to think like a scientist, Joel. And scientists naturally look for the logical solution to problems instead of those based in faith. They tend to think linearly, and so there is no room for faith in the treatment of their patients. But when all treatments have failed, who do the doctors call in for the last rites? Men of faith. Is it so hard to believe that someone might have a special gift of faith that you—a trained psychiatrist—might not understand?"

"I suppose it shouldn't be that hard to believe," Joel answered. Perhaps that is what motivated me to begin Project Séance. That is really why I came to talk to you."

Then Joel discussed how he forgot about the project because he thought it was a flop. That's when he started working with Tunisha.

"At first, I thought—maybe I hoped—these were spirits trying to contact people. But now I don't know what these are. What do you think?"

"Well, considering my philosophy on the state of the dead, I would think they were demons."

"Demons?"

"Sure, why not. Think about it, Joel. Say a demon is trying to get you to kill yourself. He's not gonna be saying, 'Hey come on over to the dark side and off yourself. There's plenty of misery and pain and fire for everybody. No, he's gonna pretend to be somebody you trust. And he's gonna say everybody dead is just livin' it up—like being dead is one big party, right? Listen, Joel," continued Pastor Jackson, "You believe in God? Tell me, do you believe in God?"

"Yes."

"Pretty much every religion teaches God is everywhere, in everything, right?"

"Yeah."

"Well, demons are everywhere, too. They are all over us, watching us."

Joel considered everything the pastor had said.

"But look, Joel. What *I* believe is not the issue. It's what *you* choose to believe. This is *your* project. Tunisha is *your* patient. Tell me. How long have you been a psychiatrist?"

"Thirty-one years," Joel answered.

"Why did you get into psychiatry? To help people, right?"

"Yes."

"What about Tunisha and the patients you are treating? You don't *want* people to kill themselves, do you? That is clearly not why you chose to do this for a living."

"Of course, not."

"Well then, I don't think it much matters what *I* think. True, maybe I'm wrong. Maybe you can really talk to Elsa, who knows? But the longer you let this project go its merry way, the more people will be hurt—regardless of whether it's spirits or demons or who knows what."

"So, if these are demons—how do you suggest I rid my system of them? An exorcism?"

The Pastor rubbed his chin for a moment. "Well now, I'm going to propose a logical and scientific solution to a supernatural dilemma. Maybe you could start by just pulling the plug."

Joel had decided after his discussion with the preacher that this was exactly what he would do. He would simply terminate Project Séance and pull the plug.

Chapter 23- Pulling the Plug

After meeting with Pastor Jackson at the fellowship luncheon in the Central Saint Louis Seventh Day Adventist Church one Saturday morning, Dr. Joel Russell decided to terminate Project Séance. He left the church and immediately drove to the site of his laboratory, located on the third floor of one of the buildings in a complex formerly known as the Old Lemp Brewery. Having acknowledged that his project was now the site of some uncommon supernatural occurrences, he was uncertain as to the exact source of the communications being made through the project. He had avoided going there since he discovered this activity going on over a week ago. In reality, he had been too afraid of what he might find if he returned.

Dr. Russell's project was a groundbreaking discovery, uniquely one of a kind. But after discussing the subject at length with Pastor Jackson, he concluded that—for the safety and well-being of the living—the project must be dismantled and never discussed with anyone. As a physician who had committed his life's work to human service, he knew that, if he allowed Project Séance to continue, he would be undoing everything good he strived to achieve during his lifetime.

Joel approached the massive, locked door to Project Séance. From inside, he could hear knocking noises and the sound of loud thumps. He could also faintly hear the television and piano. He hesitantly entered the security code and pushed open the heavy door. There he saw even more of a flurry of activity than he had the previous week. In the sitting room, the rockers were still rocking. The television switched channels as the volume vacillated between loud and soft. The pages to books, different from the books which lay on the Rococo desk last week, were still flipping.

Joel walked over to the player piano, which was playing a ragtime tune, Scott Joplin's *Maple Leaf Rag*. Thinking at first that a roll had been loaded to play, he realized, not only had the roll loaded there reached its end, but it was an entirely different tune than the tune currently playing. And whoever played this song would make an occasional mistake. When he approached the empty piano bench, he felt a sudden chill, and an extreme feeling of nausea overtook him. He moved away.

He turned toward the computer stations located at the heart of his project. The monitors were flashing, sensors were blinking, and lines of messages were printing across each screen more furiously and faster than before. The printers, upon which he had loaded several reams of paper the previous week, were completely exhausted of supplies and had been empty for some time.

Joel reached over to the top sheet, laying upside down on the first laser printer. This page had printed out several days before and had several messages typed on it. Who were these entities and what were they trying to say? Joel read the page before him. The messages, listed one by one, read almost like a report from an underworld Western Union telegraph office. Each message meant something to someone somewhere, but Joel had no idea what any of them meant.

Annabelle,

I hid the $500 under a loose floorboard in the upstairs bathroom. Take the money and buy yourself a new horse and seed for the farming season. I won't be back for planting, so you'll have to hire a man to do some of the work for you.

Love, Roger

Roger_ Smith02181883

To My Darling Son Alvin,

I am sorry that you had to discover me with my head in a noose. I had been suffering for some time, and I didn't know how to talk to your father anymore. Please don't be angry at me. I love you, and I hope you can move on with your life. Be happy.

Love, Momma

Emma_Jones04051959

Hello Cheekie,

I think I went a little too heavy on the heroin after the concert. What a trip this has been! You should try it. It's really heavy, man. Really heavy.

Jim

James_Laughlin10021971

Sergeant Jake Sternen,

Hey, Jakie! Still blowing things up?

We're dead and lovin' it.

Your buddies PB&J

Paul_Drake04112002

Wait, Joel thought. He reread the last message twice more. *This message is for Jake Sternen!* Joel looked at the email address where the message had been sent, but he didn't recognize the recipient as Jake. *Who was this message sent to? Jake? Where was Jake? Had he seen this?*

Joel again felt sick to his stomach. Reading the last page and the message for Jake Sternen made him realize that the time had come to pull the plug on this project *now*. How many of these people received these messages? He couldn't even comprehend it all. "This shit has got to stop now!" he said out loud to himself and whoever was in the room.

With that final thought, Joel didn't stop to archive anything or power anything down. He headed toward the front of the room to the right of the security door. There, still inside the room and just to the right of the door, was a locked breaker box which supplied power to his entire project. Joel pulled out his key, unlocked the breaker box and flipped every breaker to the off position. The computers and television gave out a final "ping", and then everything stopped. All the lights went off. Everything was silent.

He then walked back into the darkened room and reached for every exposed electrical cord and surge protector and yanked each of them out of the wall. He tore every camera and sensor off its mount and dashed them to the floor. He was clearly angry at something—someone—he didn't know. And he took out all of his anger and pent up frustrations on the equipment in the room.

During his rage, Joel was tormented by a flurry of images from his past. He thought about Marta Kennison, lying dead in her home in Chesterfield. He thought about Joanna and how upset she was to have received Marta's email. He considered poor Tunisha, lying unconscious in a pool of her own blood on her bathroom floor. And he thought about his poor Elsa, incinerated in the blast Jake had set eight years ago.

He picked up a rocker and threw it at the television monitor, knocking it to the ground. He grabbed a copy of *Huckleberry Finn* lying open on its spine on the Rococo desk and tore all its pages out, tossing them on the floor in front of him.

As he picked up items, ripping them off the wall and destroying them, he was consumed with an overwhelming sense of guilt and loss, anger, and self-pity. And he took all his frustrations out on the objects in the room, simply because they were the nearest things available to him. *Who are these people that they feel the need to toy with the living?* Fortunately, no living human being was present to witness the level of violence to which Dr. Russell had been provoked. He wasn't a violent man, but if he could flatten the person or entity responsible for this mess, he would.

Then, he stopped for a moment as he realized the truth of his situation. *It is me. I am responsible for all this. This is all **my** doing.*

Finally, calming himself, Joel stood for a moment. And, in the pitch darkness of the room now in disarray, Dr. Russell grabbed what he could see of the computer printouts and locked the front door, leaving Project Séance far behind him.

Chapter 24- Message to Jake

Joel Russell sat in the living room of his Dogtown rental home, reviewing the reams and reams of paper filled with cryptic messages from beyond for unknown recipients. None of these messages, except for one, had any meaning to him. That was the message for Jake Sternen. What did it mean, and did he ever receive it?

It had been over a year since Jake escaped from the prison mental hospital. No one seemed to know Jake's whereabouts. Yet, whoever sent this message seemed to know where he was. Maybe he could email this address and get in touch with Jake.

Then Joel remembered more about Jake and his initial meeting with him at St. John's Hospital. He recalled how insistent Jake was to talk to him—and only him. He recalled his first meeting with Jake and how he insisted that God had instructed him "to prevent Doctor Russell from doing something horrible". But at the time, Joel had dismissed him as being completely delusional.

He thought for a moment. *That's right. I kept my session tapes. Shit, where are they?* Joel first struggled to find the box, still packed, filled with his office contents, which Joanna had packed for him. He pulled out the framed diplomas and books to find a mini-tape recorder at the bottom. *Tape—where's that tape?* He fumbled through the small cassettes until he found one marked, "Jake Sternen 02/02/03". *That's it. He put the tape in the old recorder, but it wouldn't play. Shit.....Batteries. Where are the batteries?* He dug around in the box again and found an unused box of batteries. He doubted that they even worked anymore, but he would give it a try. He opened the box and pulled out two. He pressed the play button and fell back on the sofa, holding the recorder in his palm.

Joel's recognized his own voice on the tape.

"This is Doctor Joel Russell, and I am here with Jake Sternen. Jake, I just wanted to let you know that I am taping this session. Are you okay with that?"

"Sure, Doc."

Joel remembered that Jake had referred to him as "Doc".

"Now, Jake, I understand you were a Sergeant in the Army, is that correct?"

"Yes, that's right. I was stationed in Afghanistan during Operation Enduring Freedom."

"And what is it that you were doing in Afghanistan?"

"It was my first tour of duty. I was EOD, Explosive Ordinance Disposal. My job was to render bombs safe for disposal."

"I understand that you suffered a traumatic brain injury, which resulted from an IED explosion, is that correct?"

"Yes, the whole mission was just one big Charlie Foxtrot."

Joel sat puzzled.

Jake explained what that meant to Dr. Russell.

"That's a cluster fuck! It was a disaster!"

"Tell me more"

"Well, I don't really want to talk about that."

"Why not?"

Jake was silent.

Joel continued his interview.

"Is it true that you were discharged because of your injuries?"

"Yeah. They thought it made me crazy. They said I had lost touch with reality."

"You think they're wrong?"

"Hell yeah! I'm not fuckin' crazy, Doc."

"Tell me, Jake, why are you here? Why don't you get help at the VA Hospital?"

"Because they're all a bunch of foreign hacks who can barely speak English. All they wanna do is put you down with drugs. Some even say they *want to shock the shit out of you! Plus, I'm not fuckin' crazy."*

"Yet you came here. Perhaps you think you need some kind of help? The Intake Specialist stated that, when she interviewed you at your admission, you demanded to see me. Why is that?"

"Look, Doc. Ever since the explosion—you know, where my buddies were killed—I have been able to see things."

"See things? Like what?"

"It's like I have special powers. I can see into the future. Only, it's all mixed up with the past. So, I see the future in the past. It's like it's all happening at once, and I can't keep them straight, you know? I mean, I can see how it does sound crazy, but I'm not crazy. I just have these special powers. Ever since—you know—boom!"

Jake mimicked an explosion at his right temple by opening his fist, widening his eyes with a look of surprise.

"These assholes at the VA—they don't believe me. They try to say I'm crazy, but I'm tellin' you—I'm not fuckin' crazy!"

"I didn't say you were crazy. So tell me, why is it that you insisted on seeing me, in particular?"

"Well, you know, after the explosion—where my three buddies were killed—I was real de-

pressed. I felt guilty that I was the only one who survived. And I tried to figure out why God spared me and the other guys were all killed. And I figured it out. I believe God saved my life because he has sent me on a special mission."

"Special mission?"

"Yes, Doc. He wants me to stop you from doing what you're about to do."

"Is that so? And what is it that I'm about to do?"

Jake leaned forward to whisper to Joel.

"You are going to open up the gates to hell, and God wants me to stop you."

Dr. Russell remained silent.

"Did you hear what I said? That's why I needed to see you. God sent me here to stop you. What d'you think about that?"

Joel paused for a moment, trying to craft a well-thought response.

"I think you need help, Jake. I think your doctors at the VA are right. I'm inclined to agree with their diagnosis of PTSD. And I do think you are delusional. You clearly suffer from post-war trauma, and I'm not nearly as well equipped to help you with that as they are. I believe we need to get you transferred there. In the meantime, I think it would help if we increase your dose of antipsychotic medication."

Upon hearing this, Jake seethed in anger. Of course, Joel could not see his expression on the audio tape, but playing it back played back the entire session in his mind, as if he were reliving it.

"You fuckin' asshole! You're just like all the rest of those fuckin' quacks, VA or not! You think you fuckin' know me, with your Ivy League education and your holier-than-thou attitude, living in your big fuckin' Clayton mansion and driving your stupid Lexus. But, you don't know SHIT! I'm telling you that I have a gift, goddam it! And I'm gonna stop you, asshole. I promise!"

Jake had become so loud that the staff outside Joel's office could hear him screaming. A psych tech knocked on Joel's door, and Joel could hear his voice on the tape.

"Doctor Russell, do you need some assistance here?"

"Yes," Joel replied.

Jake, seeing that staff members had come to remove him from Dr. Russell's office, became even more enraged.

"Keep your fuckin' hands off me!"

He turned to Joel.

"I'm warning you, asshole. I'm gonna have to stop you, before you and Priya open the goddam gates to hell!"

By this time, three techs had entered the room and placed Jake face down on the floor.

"You asshole! You're all fuckin' assholes!"

For a few moments on the tape, Joel could hear a scuffle, but no conversation. The techs were removing Jake from the office and taking him down to seclusion. After Jake had been taken down the hallway, a psychiatric nurse walked in. Joel spoke to her.

"Let's up his Risperdal to 18 milligrams per day and see how that goes. And we need to check with Social Services to get him transferred to the VA as soon as possible."

There was thirty seconds of silence, followed by the sound of a large click, as Joel turned off the recorder.

Listening to the recording, it occurred to Joel that, even though he had forgotten this initial interview with Jake, it now seemed so real—as if it happened yesterday. But now, he noticed something important while listening to it, and he rewound the tape to replay it.

"I'm warning you, asshole. I'm gonna have to stop you, before you and Priya open the goddam gates to hell!"

Joel stopped the tape. Priya? How did Jake know about Priya? Not even Joel knew Priya at that time. They had opened up the gates to hell? What was Jake referring to—Project Séance? If these spirits were not really spirits but demons, then he *had* opened up the gates to hell. If Jackson was right, Joel had enabled demons to communicate with the living, deceiving them into thinking that being dead was, as Pastor Jackson had called it—one "big old party".

When he replayed this session over and over, a sudden feeling of terror filled Dr. Russell as he realized that, perhaps, Jake was right. Maybe God did spare him to prevent Joel from "opening the gates to hell."

But the project was dead now, a thing of the past. Although he was unsure of how much damage it had caused and how many lives it had affected, he did know that it did impact poor Tunisha's life. And it scared the living hell out of Joanna.

Joel couldn't fathom the idea that, if Jake was spared by God to prevent him and Priya from opening the gates to hell by launching Project Séance, why then, did God take Elsa but spare him?

Chapter 25- "The Canary Lives"

It had been a week since Joel Russell had abandoned Project Séance. His patient, Tunisha, had been discharged from the hospital and returned to the youth center, trying to resume her normal activities. It was the first day of December, and Joel also seemed to be moving on.

He had spent the Thanksgiving holiday working and trying to distract himself from the loneliness that went along with being a widower with no children. Although his work seemed to keep him going and gave him reason to continue, he understood why many of his patients had a difficult time with the holidays. He was no exception. It seemed the cold air, the television, and every sign in every store window seemed to cry out "Loser!" to anyone who didn't have someone to spend the holidays with.

This morning, he sat at home at his desk in the living room, perched in front of his computer. It was Saturday. He woke up and sat before the computer monitor in his boxers, reading his email. Rubbing his hands together, he blew into his palms. *It's rather cold in here,* he thought to himself. *As soon as I read my email, I'll jump in the shower and turn up the heat.* He looked through his inbox, now overflowing with new email messages. *I really need a better spam blocker,* he thought. *Let's see what I can delete without reading. Scanning. . . . scanning . . . delete . . scanning....*

Suddenly he gasped, as he discovered there, in his email inbox, a new message from

Elsa_Russell06042003@projectseance.com.

Joel was struck by a sudden sense of panic. He hesitated, contemplating several minutes, before finally deciding to open the email message.

> *Dr. Joel Russell, M.D.,*
>
> *It has been quite some time since we last saw each other, and I'm afraid to admit that we did not part on very good terms. For that, I believe I owe you an apology.*
>
> *I confess that I had suspected something had been going on between you and Joanna for some time. But for a long time, I was simply in denial about it. I was afraid to admit to myself that I felt insecure about our relationship. At times, I was even jealous of Joanna. She possessed every quality I didn't. She had beauty, success, intelligence, youth, and those wide, childbearing hips. I feared that you would leave me for a woman who could both satisfy your desires and perhaps bear you the children I never could. I had nothing to offer you, Joel. I felt that if I confronted you about the affair, you would most certainly leave me.*

Joel, please know that I have never loved anyone but you. You were my soulmate, my lover, my world. I only hope that you can forgive me for ignoring your feelings and desires.

By the way, Dr. Russell, also know this—the canary lives.

Your loving wife,

Elsa

Joel was shocked. Elsa had tried to contact him. And she used the project as a means to communicate. *This has to be Elsa.* She always called Joel by his full name and title. And she often joked in passing about Joanna's "childbearing hips". Plus, no one else knew the code words that they had discussed in the garden that day. *This had to be Elsa,* Joel kept thinking to himself.

But then he began thinking. *What was the date of this email? Yesterday? That can't be......*

Joel had pulled the plug on Project Séance over a week ago.

Initially, Joel sat in a stupor in front of his computer monitor. Then, he abruptly got up, hastily dressed himself, and then ran out of his front door. Although it was a cold December day in Saint Louis, the doctor didn't stop to grab an overcoat. He just headed out to his car.

The trip from his Dogtown house to the brewery was a blur, partly because he was speeding and partly because he kept replaying Elsa's email in his mind. He was trying to sort things through.

The email had yesterday's date. Joel halted the project last week. Therefore, someone must have reactivated the project. But no one, aside from Priya and Pastor Jackson knew what the project was about.

As he traversed the highway and the many back streets of South Saint Louis, he thought of Elsa. She knew about Joanna? Why was *she* sorry? It was *he* who cheated on *her*. It had to be Elsa, he thought. The message included their agreed upon secret code, "The canary lives." Plus, she addressed him by his full name, a name she had used for him ever since their first encounter. And the reference to Joanna's "childbearing hips" was unmistakably Elsa's.

This couldn't be demons. This had to be Elsa's spirit, trying to communicate with Joel. This is why he wanted to launch Project Séance in the first place. He wanted to talk to her and tell her how sorry he was for having wounded her so deeply. He never had the chance to tell her that in life, because her life was so tragically cut short.

Soon he arrived at the brewery. Because it was Saturday, there were quite a few bands inside practicing. As Joel ascended the stairs to the second floor, he saw Ariel standing there. She looked surprised to see him and shook her head in a sort of double-take.

"Wait….Did you just get here?" she asked.

"Yeah, why."

"Well, I thought you were upstairs playing the piano."

"No. Has someone been playing the piano?"

"Yes, all day. And making a ton of racket. The noise is horrendous." She paused. "Joel, what's been going on? Hey, does this have something to do with Joanna's two patients who offed themselves this week? Bruce says you've got some kind of a freaky lab up there. Last week, when she was pissed at you, you took my key and came back here. That was the last anyone saw of you."

"Hold on. Did you just say Joanna had patients who killed themselves last week?"

"Yeah. One hanged herself, and the other guy shot himself in the head. Joel, don't you watch the news?"

Joel had not told Ariel anything about Project Séance. But she looked straight at him. "I know there is something bad going on up there, Joel. There's just this awful feeling I've been getting since you moved in upstairs. I can't tell you exactly what it is, but I just get this terrible feeling like I'm surrounded by pure evil."

Joel grabbed Ariel's hand and ran with her through the hallway and up the steps to the third floor, punching in his security code. He hesitantly pushed in the massive door. As Joel cracked the door he could see blinding lights shining throughout the room. When he opened the door, a whoosh of light and ice cold air forced its way out of the room and through their bodies, chilling them.

They both stood at the doorway. Joel glanced back at Ariel to see a look of terror on her face. "Holy crap!" she cried.

"I don't understand!" Joel screamed. "I unplugged all this shit last week. How could this be?"

Ariel's feet were frozen in place. She stood, in shock. "What the hell is this?"

Joel used his key to unlock the breaker box, located just inside the front door. Each switch had been flipped to the "off" position as Joel had left it. "I just don't understand. What the hell?"

"Oh, my God......I think I'm gonna be sick." Ariel leaned against the door and bent over to vomit.

He moved into the room. All the while Ariel stood in the hallway outside. Joel ran in to see that the computers were on and working, and messages were still being typed even faster than before. Someone was keying in these messages faster than was humanly possible!

Joel reached behind one of the computers to again pull the plug. The plug, too, remained as he had left it—still unplugged. As he surveyed the room, he realized that every plug for every piece of electronic equipment had been pulled out of the wall. Yet something supernatural now energized all this equipment in the laboratory!

The piano played very brusquely and loudly. The rocking chairs rocked, and the television, still laying on its side and completely unplugged, was on, still switching from station to station. When Joel peered over to the antique dolls in the crib, he heard children's voices and laughter. And the pages to *Huckleberry Finn*, which he had torn out the previous week, were now hovering in circles above his head.

The overhead lights were not on, but the room was so clearly illuminated, they weren't necessary. This time—unlike any other time before—Joel could see these illuminated shadows of figures. These were people from all walks of life, all ages, from different periods in time. He would feel a sudden chill, accompanied by an extreme feeling of nausea as an apparition would pass through him. And for a moment, he would be flooded with a consciousness that was not his own. It was as if these entities were passing through him, trying to channel through him.

Project Séance now had a life of its own, and Dr. Russell was still unsure of who was the true force behind it. He had tried to halt the project, but it was clear to him now that he would have to do something more drastic. Perhaps he would try talking to them. Although this was a simple solution, maybe that's all it might take. He screamed, "You need to leave now! You can't be here! I don't want you here!" He picked up a computer monitor and smashed it on the floor. He picked up a chair and threw it against the wall, breaking it into pieces.

Then, Joel watched as a heavy hardcover book propelled itself off the Rococo desk, hitting him in the head, leaving a bloody puncture wound. More items flew at him—pieces of the chair he had just broken and the cameras and sensors he had detached from the wall the previous week. They all flew at his head, striking him several times.

He heard whispering and mumbling, as these unknown entities were now telling *him* to leave. And suddenly, he felt a very strong push at his back. He could have sworn he heard a voice cry, "*You* leave!"

Joel felt himself being pushed back out into the hallway where Ariel stood. The moment he cleared the security door and was back in the hallway, Joel heard a huge sucking sound, as if all the light and energy that had spilled out into the hallway was now being sucked back into the room again. The door slammed shut behind him. He tried to reenter the code, repeating it to himself. The door wouldn't open. He tried repeatedly reentering the code. But something had obviously pushed him out into the hallway and had now locked him out.

In vain, he tried pounding and kicking on the door. Whatever or whoever remained inside clearly didn't want him there. He beat on the door, demanding to be let in. Behind the door, he could hear loud rumbling noises and the sound of deafening screams. All the while, Ariel stood at the door watching Joel, paralyzed with fear. Then, she looked up at him in panic, said nothing, and ran down the stairs and out of the building.

Standing there, locked out of the project he had once built, Dr. Joel Russell now knew that what Jake Sternen had warned him about had actually come true. *He really had opened the gates to hell.*

Chapter 26- Donation for the Homeless

It was 3 P.M. Saturday afternoon, and Joel sat alone in the living room in his Dogtown rental house, trying unsuccessfully to think up a solution to end the chaos which had erupted in his laboratory. Although Ariel had witnessed the most recent incident, he didn't confide in her any of his secrets regarding the project—about Tunisha's message from Tony, about the message for Jake, or the one from Elsa. Moreover, Joel knew that, without having talked directly to Joanna in detail, that his project had somehow played a role in the suicides of both her patients last week. Project Séance had been undoubtedly commandeered by an unknown force, much more powerful than he was. He would not only have to keep this project's existence and purpose confidential, he would have to enlist the help of an expert to identify and destroy its existence—before *it* destroyed any more lives.

Of course, he couldn't confide any of this to Joanna. Yes, they had a history, but she was also his colleague. And he couldn't trust any colleague to believe his story. He didn't blame her for that. He knew that, if the shoe were on the other foot—if *she* were telling *him* such a wild story—he would also never believe her. He would dismiss her just as he did poor Jake Sternen. He would—in a very professional manner—call her crazy.

He considered all these things as he drove the highway to Grand Avenue. It was time for Saturday evening mass, and he needed to find a priest. During the time he practiced psychiatry in Saint Louis and also during many social events he attended while married to Elsa, Joel met several priests who taught at Saint Louis University and had parishes downtown. Joel was not a Catholic, but he had decided, *It is now time for me to see a priest.*

It seemed every time Dr. Russell made the trip off of Highway 40 onto a major exit downtown, there was always a homeless person panhandling for spare change. Not that he really seemed to mind. He had worked with many homeless people before, and it didn't bother him to hand out a few bucks through his car window while the light turned red. This afternoon, he had turned off of Highway 40 to go north on Grand Avenue, which ran through the Saint Louis University Campus, a Jesuit university. Also, this section of town was not far from the Saint Louis Cathedral Basilica on Lindell.

Joel's car was several cars behind a line of cars, stopped at the red light and waiting to turn onto Grand. He was not surprised to see a homeless man standing at the red light, holding a large paper cup in his right hand. In his left, he held a cardboard sign, which said, "Homeless Veteran. Hungry." The man had long hair and an unruly beard. He wore torn

179

jeans, a plaid flannel shirt, and a knit winter cap. His windbreaker was worn and much too thin for the month of December. He was shivering.

Joel thought nothing of reaching into his wool coat pocket to pull out some loose bills he had put there. He found a $5.00 bill and opened his window, flagging the homeless man down. The man noticed Dr. Russell's signals and approached him. Then, the man seemed to recognize him and stopped short.

Joel, in turn, recognized the homeless man as Jake Sternen. He looked emaciated, and he had grown his hair and beard. He looked as if he truly hadn't eaten a good meal in some time, but Joel knew that it was definitely Jake. And, when Jake realized that Joel had recognized him, he dropped his cup and his sign and ran.

It's Jake, he thought. *I've got to talk to Jake!* He jumped out of his car, leaving the engine running and the door wide open and ran after Jake. "Jake, stop! Jake! I need to talk to you! Jake!"

Jake continued to run, and Joel continued after him. Although he was not necessarily a faster runner than Jake, Jake's shoes were worn and falling apart. His soles were duct taped to his shoes, and they had hindered his ability to run very fast. Dr. Russell grabbed him by the shoulders and pushed him to the ground, falling behind him.

Jake got up and started to run again. So this time, Joel grabbed him by the shoulders, twisting him around, and pinned him up against a nearby wall.

Joel had never attacked another man in his life. But today, Joel was not himself. "Jake, you have to talk to me!" he pleaded.

"Leave me the fuck alone, man!" Jake was livid and practically spitting in Joel's face.

"No, listen to me, Jake! How did you know about Priya?"

"I don't know what the fuck you're talkin' about, man!"

"You know, Project Séance? 'The gates of hell'? How did you know about Priya?" Joel demanded.

Jake spat out each word, enunciating them as if he thought Joel was stupid. "Look, I told you—I don't know what the fuck you're talkin' about! Now, leave me the fuck alone!" Jake tried to push Joel out of his way.

"Bullshit!" Joel pinned him up against the wall even more forcefully. "You were telling me about the future. You were telling me about Priya and the Project eight years before it happened."

"What?"

"Look, Jake. I need your help. You gotta help. There is nobody else. *Nobody.* You've got to help me destroy it!"

Jake had had enough. He punched Joel repeatedly before he fell to the ground. "Leave me alone, you fuckin' psycho! You know *you're* the fuckin' psycho, not *me*! Do you have any idea how long it took me to realize there's nothing—nothing I can do??? This shit has ruined my life, and I realize—you know what? It doesn't matter. *You can't change the future any more than you can change the past.* And, you know what else? I don't give a fuck anymore!"

By this time, the stoplight to Grand Avenue had turned green. Joel's car had blocked traffic, and frustrated drivers behind him were honking their horns. A well-dressed man had witnessed the entire scene and got out of his car to help Dr. Russell, after he saw Jake strike him. He pulled Jake away and asked Joel if he was alright. Jake glared at the intervening stranger.

"Oh, so you're protecting *him* from *me*? What a joke! *He's* the fuckin' psycho!" Jake began walking away and turned again toward Joel, while he lay on the ground, rubbing his cheek. "And don't fuckin' follow me, or I will—I'll fuckin' kill you!" He turned away again and walked off.

"Who's PB&J, Jake?" Joel asked.

Jake stopped but did not turn around.

"I have a message from Paul Drake. 'Dead and lovin' it. Signed, PB&J.'"

Jake had his back to Joel, who still sat on the ground, rubbing his wounds. Joel could hear him whispering something softly but inaudibly to himself, as he looked down at his feet. Then, Jake came to his senses and darted off.

The Samaritan extended a hand to help Dr. Russell to his feet, as Jake disappeared behind a Saint Louis University campus building, out of sight.

Joel returned to his car, wiping his bloody lip. Some of the drivers stopped several cars behind him and opened their windows to survey the cause for the traffic jam. The light at Grand Avenue had changed several times since Joel had chased after Jake. A few irate drivers and passengers screamed at Joel, as he returned to his car and moved it out of the way of traffic. He pulled it off to the side of Grand Avenue, thinking to himself, while he kept the motor running. The angry drivers who had been held up maneuvered around Joel's parked car and screamed one last flurry of obscenities before passing him on the left. Most of the irritated drivers just glared at Joel with an evil look as they passed him, before once again speeding off to their intended destinations.

Dr. Russell decided to pull out into traffic and see if he could find Jake. He couldn't have gone too far too quickly. *After all, he can't run very fast with his shoes duct taped together*, he thought to himself.

Joel took numerous side trips through the back alleys around campus, up and down Grand Avenue, East and West on Laclede Avenue, and down every one way street and behind every building in the vicinity. He even looked behind several dumpsters, hoping Jake might be hiding behind them, seeking shelter from the cold.

Finally, after one hour of desperately searching, Joel gave up. He once again steered his car north on Grand Avenue, turning westward onto Lindell Boulevard. It was almost 5 P.M. He headed toward the Central West End, because he decided he needed to attend Saturday evening mass. He still needed desperately to enlist the help of a priest to help him with his current crisis of trying to halt the project. He had been initially distracted by his encounter with Jake Sternen, but Jake had fled the scene. Joel's situation was now dire, and he needed to remain focused.

He traveled several blocks West on Lindell, before parking his car alongside the street adjoining the Cathedral Basilica of Saint Louis.

The city of Saint Louis was a city of varied cultures and religious affiliations, but many of its neighborhoods were still predominantly Catholic. A plethora of Catholic churches and parishes blanketed the entire metropolitan area, but this particular building—the Cathedral Basilica—had a rich history in the city. It was the seat of the Saint Louis Archdiocese, having taking many hands and many years to complete.

Although the ground-breaking ceremony for the cathedral was held in 1907, the building itself was not officially consecrated until nineteen years later in 1926. Inlaid gold mosaics lined the entire cathedral. Massive ornate statues, an enormous altar, many intricate stained-glass windows, and countless other priceless artifacts and works of art towered above the lowly spectator, filling them with a sense of spiritual wonder and awe. Numerous artisans had devoted their entire life's work to helping erect this historic house of worship.

The massive cathedral was a combination of Romanesque and Byzantine design. As Joel approached the front of the cathedral, he was overwhelmed by its size and beauty.

This was not his first time inside the cathedral. He had visited and admired the building's interior twice on previous tours, which the Archdiocese often permitted for the benefit of the general public. But Joel had never attended this church in order to worship. This time, as Joel entered the colossal front doors of the cathedral and walked through the narthex, he felt a hallowed sense of serenity as he studied the countless mosaic images depicted on every length of wall, floor, and ceiling.

He reverently and quietly followed the other parishioners into the sanctuary. Each church member paused at the font of holy water and at their respective pews, kneeling and making the sign of the cross. Although he maintained his reverent demeanor, he didn't engage in this practice. He simply seated himself in the far rear, right corner pew, trying not to stand out. The other parishioners knew he was not Catholic, but they didn't seem to perceive him as an intruder.

The sanctuary was filled this evening, but Joel managed to sit sufficiently far enough in the back to establish a comfortable amount of space around himself in the pew, thereby avoiding having to sit too close to other members of the congregation. Occasionally, a stranger would make eye contact and smile, but this was only a passing gesture, and he never felt compelled to introduce himself or make pleasant conversation.

As the mass commenced, Joel realized he was clearly out of his element. He felt completely unfamiliar with the numerous rituals, gestures, and responses required of him during the service. He did master the system of hymns and responses, finally getting a feel for who should sing and when. But for the most part, if he didn't know what to do, he didn't do anything. His eyes were transfixed on the enormous and ornate altar ahead and the priests conducting the mass.

As the communion ceremony commenced, Joel remained seated in his pew. Each row of parishioners filed out to partake of the wine and bread, lining up efficiently and neatly into long rows. Each participating member would partake of the Blood and Body of Christ, walking past the priests, and winding back around to return to their seats. Joel was impressed with how quickly this all took place for such a huge congregation. Compared to other churches' communion services he had attended, the priests had streamlined this communion service thoroughly and efficiently.

As Joel waited for the participants to finish the communion portion of the service, he heard a "Psst" from the pew behind him. He didn't check behind him to see who was whispering. He was obviously not a member there. He knew no one there, so he ignored the noise, keeping his eyes fixed forward.

"Psst! Hey Doc," Joel heard coming from behind. This time, he noted a very acrid stench emanating from the pew behind him. He knew it was Jake Sternen, who was seated behind him. The woman seated next to Joel scowled at him disapprovingly.

Joel turned around to acknowledge Jake. "Jake! What are doing? Did you follow me here?"

"Yeah, Doc." Jake stood up, and moved up to Joel's pew, sitting between Joel and the disapproving woman next to him. She reluctantly moved away, and Joel could sense that Jake's enveloping stench repelled her. She wiggled her nose and frowned.

"Paul, Butch and Josh," Jake whispered loudly to Joel.

"What?" Joel asked, puzzled.

"That's PB&J—Paul, Butch, and Josh. My buddies who were killed in Kandahar. You know, that message you received for me?" Jake whispered, but he could still be heard several pews in either direction.

"Jake! Where the hell did you go? I looked all over for you." Joel whispered, trying to be quiet.

An irritated parishioner turned around to "shush" Joel.

"You really did it, didn't you Doc? You really did get their message?" Jake asked.

Joel tried to avoid creating a scene. Even though he wasn't a Catholic and he currently had a bruised cheek and bleeding lip, Joel could still easily slink around in this part of town unnoticed. But Jake stood out wherever he went, even when he tried to be discreet and blend in with the crowd. Joel knew that, if he didn't remove Jake from the sanctuary soon, he would have even more irate worshipers—possibly the whole congregation and the priests—all turning around and shushing him.

Joel grabbed Jake by the shoulder, placing his index finger over his mouth and quietly leading him out of the sanctuary back into the narthex. He led him out the front doors and stood on the front steps of the cathedral, facing him. He needed to explain himself, and whispering his point would not get it across to him.

"Look, Jake....I know that you didn't mean to kill Elsa. You meant to kill me. And, I'm telling you now—I believe you. This thing—" He choked. "You're right Jake. I *have* opened the gates to hell. And I believe that only *you* can help me close them. I don't know how to do it. Believe me, I've already tried to unplug it and cut off the power. But this thing is more that I can handle now. That's why I came here. I was looking for a priest to help. Hell, I'm not even Catholic, but, quite frankly, I have run out of options." Joel entreated Jake for a response.

Jake stood for a minute, considering everything that Joel had been trying to tell him. Then he smiled and nodded, patting Dr. Russell on the arm. "You don't need a priest, Doc. You have *me*. That's why I'm here. You *need* me. *I'll* help you."

"Seriously? I'm still not sure how to get myself out of this mess. Listen, Jake. I'm really glad I found you," Joel commented, relieved.

"Sure, Doc. *You* found *me*," Jake sarcastically agreed. "Really, I'll do whatever you say."

He quickly changed the subject. "Say, you wouldn't still happen to have that fiver you were going to give me before? I'm starved."

"You can come back to my place." Joel responded. He and Jake walked side by side back to Joel's car. "But first, you've *got* to take a shower. You're pretty ripe."

"Ripe?" Jake smelled his armpit. "I hadn't noticed, Doc. I think maybe you're just a little too picky about the company you keep. You'd probably have more friends if you weren't such a snob."

"Oh, is that so?" Joel chuckled.

"Yeah, Doc. You gotta really work on your people skills. I could give you some pointers."

"I'll bet you knew all along that I was coming for you, didn't you?" Joel asked.

"Well, yeah, Doc. I did."

"Then why did you hit me?" Joel asked, rubbing his chin.

"I was just playing with you, Doc. Really, I was holding back. I could've really fucked you up if I meant to. And, pretty much, you deserved it."

"I see. Well, thanks for putting on the kid gloves," Joel stated, moving his sore lower jaw from left to right. He looked seriously at Jake. "Why did you come back for me, Jake?"

"I guess I figured, even if I can't change the future, I've got nothing to lose by helping you. It's not like I've got a job or a home or any money or a girl—or even a life. At least, if I give this a shot, I can hang with my BFF and maybe get a free meal out of the deal." Jake grinned, put his arm on Joel's shoulder, and escorted him back to his car.

Chapter 27- Joanna's Discovery

After finding Jake Sternen on the streets and convincing him to help devise a plan to dismantle Project Séance, Joel Russell escorted Jake back to his Dogtown home.

When he and Jake returned to his house, he discovered that Joanna had been waiting for him in his living room. It seemed she had spoken to Ariel after the incident which occurred earlier that day at the brewery. Ariel didn't really know what had actually transpired, but she indicated that Joel had been involved in the episode. So, Joanna decided to come over to talk to him. She let herself in the house, since Joel had left the front door wide open in his haste to find himself a priest. Instead, his plans had been diverted, and he came home with Jake.

She was killing time during Joel's absence, and he noticed that she had picked up the project papers he left on the coffee table. She read these email printouts Joel took with him, when he initially shut down the laboratory. She realized that Joel had more involvement in the entire chain of events than he let on, and she became infuriated. He and Jake were joking as they walked in the door. She was still reading the documents, seated on the old living room sofa.

She lifted up the papers to show him. "What's this?" she demanded. "This is all you, isn't it—this Project Séance crap? This is all *your* doing, Joel?"

"I was going to tell you about this, but I wasn't sure you would believe me. Joanna, just let me explain—"

"—I don't think you need to explain! This www.projectseance.com—this is your web site? You sent the email from Marta after all. And this other crap. What's this, Joel? Fake emails from Elsa? This message from Emma Jones? Joel, do you know her son Alvin shot himself this week?"

Joel stood silent, trying to fashion an acceptable explanation for Joanna. "No, you don't understand. This isn't me. Well—yeah—I started this whole thing. But I think these are really messages from dead people or demons or—I don't really know what! I swear, Joanna—I didn't make this up!"

"Ooooh, Doc," Jake interjected, fanning himself and referring to Joanna. "Niiiiiice," he joked.

"And who the hell is this?" she snapped and pointed to Jake.

"This is Jake Sternen. Jake Sternen, Joanna Watson."

Jake extended his hand to shake hers. "Nice to meet you, little lady."

Joanna ignored Jake. "Jake Sternen? The Jake who killed Elsa? What the hell, Joel? How long have you been hanging out with him?"

"Really. I just met him on the street just now. I haven't seen him in eight years," Joel explained.

Joanna shook her head in disbelief and stood up, tossing the project papers down on the coffee table. "Oh my God, you and Jake have been into this thing this whole time. You have been sucked into this delusion of his!"

"Hey! I am *not* delusional!" Jake screamed at her.

"Well, if you're not, then you guys have been working together from the very beginning, since he killed..." Joanna's eyes widened in terror.

Joel moved toward her. "No, Joanna. It's not what you think. Really. Just give me the chance to show you. I need to explain...."

She cringed in horror, thinking Joel had masterminded not only the fake emails, but possibly Elsa's death. "Don't touch me!" She backed away, stumbling past the arm of the sofa. She grabbed her purse and ran for the front door.

"Please Joanna."

"No, Joel. You're sick. You need help. Oh, my God. I can't believe what I'm seeing right now." She ran out the front door to her car.

Joel stood at the door and screamed to her, "Joanna!"

"So, Doc....you *did* her?" Jake asked as he watched Joanna from behind.

"Once upon a time," Joel responded. He didn't say any more. He just stood at the open door, watching her leave.

"I bet she had you on a short leash, eh? I'll bet Doc was a little whipped."

"Shut up, Jake."

"Aren't you gonna go after her?" Jake asked.

"No. It's too late for that. Right now, we need to come up with a plan to end this thing. I've got to call Priya."

Priya had agreed to meet Joel and Jake at a local Waffle House restaurant at midnight. Jake had decided on the spot, partly because it was one of the few grills still open at midnight, but also because he liked the coffee there. Hungry, Jake ordered one of everything on the menu.

Jake studied the short order cook fry up the order they had placed. "I like this place, because you can see the cooks cook your food. That way, you know they're not back there spitting in it before they serve it to you."

"Yeah, that's always a problem for me, when I eat out." Joel was being sarcastic. He didn't usually frequent the Waffle House. He didn't really eat out much at all.

"So, what's been going on, Joel? I haven't heard from you since the baby shower. And suddenly you call me in hysterics about the project? What's this all about?" Priya asked.

Joel recounted to Priya the events of the last three months in vivid detail. He spoke of the fact that, when she had completed Project Séance, he had convinced himself that it had been a complete flop. But then, strange things started to happen. Someone or something supernatural controlled the system. He talked about his young patient Tunisha, the emails for Jake from his dead buddies, and the message from Elsa. He couldn't positively identify the force which currently possessed the system Priya had set up, but he felt that the system now had a life of its own. Whatever it was—was evil. It had locked him out and needed to be destroyed.

Then, he talked about seeing Jake on the street. He told her about his initial meeting with Jake eight years ago, and how Jake had predicted, even before Joel knew Priya, that he and she would "open the gates to hell". Doctor Russell recounted all the events of the past eight years in excruciating detail, while Jake ravenously ate everything the waitress had brought him. "He's paying," he would assure her, pointing to Joel.

"This is scary stuff, Joel. What do you want me to do?"

"There's nothing you really need to do. We're going to blow the place up," Jake said.

"What?" Joel asked incredulously, looking at Jake.

"Yeah. Isn't that why you asked me along? I'm an IED expert, and you need to blow things up, right?"

"Well, I hadn't really thought it through that well," Joel said. "I am trying to come up with a safer plan."

"Yeah, let's see. You tried to unplug it—that didn't work, right? And now you're locked out. So pretty much, all you got left is blowing the fucker up." Jake smiled and picked up an entire chocolate chip waffle with his fork, trying to shove as much of it in his mouth as possible without cutting it. Finally, he managed to fold it in fourths and fit it in. "Oh wait," he said with the waffle in his mouth. "We do need your cell phone. You have Doc on speed dial, don't' you?"

"Yes." Priya handed Jake the phone.

"Oh, and maybe we could borrow something else," Jake asked.

"Sure, what do you need?"

"We need to borrow your husband's lab coat and hospital badge," Jake said.

Joel glared at Jake.

"What?" Jake said. "We'll give it back."

It was 6 A.M. Sunday morning, and Joel and Jake approached Ariel's apartment, knocking on the door. Ariel sleepily answered her door in a short night shirt, rubbing her eyes. Her eyes were puffy, as if she had cried herself to sleep the night before.

"Hey, Joel. What are you doing here?"

"I need your help, Ariel," Joel pleaded.

"Yeah, I'm sorry. I didn't really sleep well since— well, you know. A lot has happened since yesterday. Why? What do you need?"

"Um, I wonder if you might call in sick next week."

"What? Yeah.....okay. But I'm not going back into the brewery for you. I told Aaron I wasn't going back, and he was pretty mad, so we broke up."

"What, the band or you and him?"

"Both. Who's this guy?" She pointed to Jake.

Jake got down on one knee and kissed Ariel's hand. "Pleased to meet you, woman of my dreams. I am ex-Army Sergeant Jake Sternen at your service."

Ariel pulled her hand away, horrified at the realization that she was in the presence of Elsa's killer. "Oh my God, Joel, is this *the* Jake? The one who—"

Jake seemed crushed that his attempt to introduce himself had been so bitterly stifled by Ariel's horrified rejection. He was still perched on one knee.

"Yes," Joel answered. "Ariel, I know what you're thinking. Believe me—I need his help. And I need *your* help. I'm just asking that you be patient, and I will try to explain everything."

Ariel paused for a long moment, and looked down at Jake, disgusted. "Well, come in. Let me get some clothes on!"

Joel and Jake sat, sipping coffee at Ariel's small kitchen dinette. The two had been up all night, so Ariel stood while she made them a second pot of coffee. Jake scarfed down a piece of toast, reviewing the bomb building plans with his mouth full.

Joel looked at Jake. "Didn't you just eat a couple of hours ago?" he asked.

"Hey, I think best if I have a full stomach." Jake looked up at Ariel. "Keep it comin' darlin'."

"Yes, master." She tossed another piece of toast in front of him, which landed cockeyed on his empty plate. Referring to Jake, she looked at Joel. "Why did you bring *him* here?"

"Well, back when he used to be a patient of mine, he tried to tell me that he could see into the future. I didn't believe him then, but I do now," Joel answered. "He had predicted that all this stuff with Project Séance would happen eight years ago."

"Oh well, that explains that psycho look he has." Ariel sneered at Jake and stuck out her tongue.

"What? I'm hungry! Can't a guy eat?" Jake glared back at Ariel. "Anyway, aren't *you* kind of a freak yourself? I thought you saw dead people." Jake returned Ariel's childish gesture by sticking his tongue out.

"Hey, what are we—seven? Ariel, I need Jake's military expertise, and I am asking you to trust me on this one. We need to get past our mistakes and work toward this common goal right now." Joel turned to Jake. "Since you are so adamant about blowing this place up, how do you propose we do this?"

"Well, the most practical way is going to be to get us a shitload of ANFO and just blow up the whole fucking building."

"I see. And just how do you propose to get this stuff? At the explosives convenience store?" Joel asked.

"Oh, believe me. There are places."

"Don't you have Army connections?" Joel asked.

"Well, Doc—you might remember that I'm kind of a wanted man. I would imagine if I went looking for high explosives, it might be a little hard for me to get lost in the crowd. No, you guys are going to have to help me," Jake stated.

"ANFO?" Joel asked. "Where do you plan to get some? Feed stores? Farmers?"

"Not likely. We're going to have to get some explosive grade ammonium nitrate. That would mean we need to raid a few coal mines and quarries."

"Coal mines and quarries?" Joel looked puzzled.

"Yeah, there are plenty around Saint Louis, especially in Illinois. Jeez, Doc. You don't get out of the city much do you? But there's other stuff we need to do. And, Doc, even though you have unlimited amounts of cash here, we're going to have to steal a lot of it. Okay, here's the plan."

Ariel sat down at the table, as Jake swallowed his last bite of toast. Then the three discussed his very elaborate plan to blow up Project Séance.

Chapter 28- Revisiting the Brewery

Joel worked hard to finally convince Ariel to return to the brewery. After Saturday's poltergeist, he wasn't sure *he* even wanted to go back, but he knew he had to. Having run off the previous afternoon, Ariel told Aaron she refused to go back and informed him she quit the band. Apparently, Aaron interpreted that to mean that she wanted to end their relationship as well.

But Doctor Russell could be both a charmer and a sweet talker. Ariel trusted him as she would her own father, and so she reluctantly—very reluctantly—agreed to go back with him. They drove the thirteen miles from Ariel's apartment toward the brewery together, and during the ride, Ariel confided in Joel the secrets of her recently broken heart.

Jake chimed in from the back seat. "Well, I'm glad Aaron dumped you. Now you're a free woman, and you can go out with me. I did tell you that you were the woman of my dreams." He leaned forward to whisper in her ear, while she rode in the front passenger's seat of Joel's car.

"I'd rather have my eyes gouged out with a hot poker," she responded, not looking back.

"Oooooh, now *you're* a saucy wench!" Jake laughed.

Joel let them both into the brewery. He had both keys—his and Ariel's—since he had not returned Ariel's key after he borrowed it two weeks before. He unlocked the front door, and they all stepped into the dark hallway of the brewery's ground floor. It was silent, but Ariel proceeded cautiously.

"Boo!" Jake jumped up from behind and grabbed Ariel, causing her to jump also.

She slapped him on the back of the head. "Jake, you moron! You scared the piss outta me!"

"Really," Joel interjected. "Must you two carry on like this? Knock it off! Be serious, Jake!"

Jake saluted. "Yes, Doc."

They ascended the dark, spiral staircase to the second floor. They immediately felt the building rumble. It almost felt like a mild aftershock after a previously devastating 7.9 Richter earthquake. They could soon hear muffled noises and screams, which obviously emanated from the top floor above, the site of Dr. Russell's laboratory.

Ariel stepped gingerly down the hallway. "Joel, I'm not sure I can do this," she warned.

Joel put his arm around her back and walked beside her. "We'll do it together, kiddo. I need your help." He looked back at Jake. "You too, Jake. I need your help, too."

To get to Dr. Russell's third floor laboratory from the second, one had to follow the long hallway opposite the entrance side of the building, walking past the practice rooms. Joel pointed out Ariel's practice room to Jake as they passed by. When they finally reached the end of the long hallway, they ascended the stairs to the third floor.

Ariel hesitated again. "They don't want us here, Joel."

"I know. If you want to just stand here at the bottom of the stairway, Jake and I can go up."

She thought for a moment. "No way! You guys are not leaving me down here by myself!" She ran after them.

Joel led them up the metal staircase to the massive door at the entrance to Project Séance. He keyed in the security code for good measure. Even though the room and door were reinforced, the screams and rumbles were now more evident and less muffled. Joel surmised that the cacophony was now audible throughout the building and had scared the rest of the building's inhabitants off. Besides the three who were now present—and whatever lay beyond the massive door—no other sign of life remained in the building.

The door was certainly locked. Joel tried again to no avail.

"Yah, um. It's not gonna happen, Doc. Jeez, it sounds like fuckin' Afghanistan all over behind there!

I'm tellin' you, we're gonna have to blow this whole fucker up!"

"It's not too late to find a priest," Joel suggested.

"Yah, um, Doc....I hate to break this to you, but most priests are pretty much chicken shit. I mean, you had a hard enough time talking *us* into coming up here. Do you think you're gonna talk some wimpy old dude with a heart condition into coming up here? I mean, just listen to that racket!

"I'm telling you, if we get these explosives the day after tomorrow, we can haul them up that freight elevator after we load them in the back. We can store and mix them in Ariel's practice room and set them up in a charge formation on late Wednesday night, leading them down the second floor hallway and up these stairs."

"Like the Oklahoma City bombing?" Joel asked.

Jake immediately went into a rage. "Hey—let's get one thing straight. I'm not a fuckin' baby killer!" Now visibly upset, he forcefully poked Joel in the chest as he spoke. "Don't ever compare me to him! If that fuckin' pansy-assed douchebag were still alive, I'd crush his fuckin' skull in with my bare fists!"

"Ok, calm down, Rambo," Ariel interrupted. "Don't get your camo panties all up in a wad. He's just asking a question. Get it together, moron!"

Jake backed off the doctor, collecting himself. Then he brushed Joel's shoulder. "Sorry, Doc. I kinda lost track of myself for a minute there. You see, the thing about this asshole McVeigh was that he claimed to be such a genius for masterminding the whole thing, and when it came right down to it, and you looked at his plans and everything on the internet, he was a fuckin' hack. I mean, he botched so much shit setting his cowardly terrorist plan in motion, everybody knew that he was just a moron bumpkin, no better than any Al-Qaeda dipshit. He was so stupid, he couldn't even do simple math calculations to figure out what he needed for his bomb mixtures. I'm ashamed to think he even served in the Army. He made us all look bad......fuckin' psycho whack job...."

Joel responded, calming Jake. "You don't have to explain that to me, Jake. I agree. He was a fuckin' psycho whack job. And, believe me, I know a whack job when I see one."

Jake smiled. "You know, Doc, you're such a helluva guy, I sometimes forget you're still a shrink."

The trio retreated down the stairs to Ariel's practice room. Notably, some of the instruments were still left turned on from the previous day's rehearsal. It looked as though some of the other band members had, like Ariel, also left in a hurried fashion—as if something had scared the living daylights out of them.

Jake sat and picked up Aaron's guitar, picking out a strikingly good rendition of Jimi Hendrick's version of *The Star-Spangled Banner*. Ariel seemed pleasantly surprised at Jake's talents, but she tried to act cool.

"Aaron plays better than you can," she teased. "He also plays drums."

Jake also responded coolly. "That may be so, little lady, but I'll bet you that I'm way better than he is in the sack." He winked at her.

Ariel smiled and said nothing.

Joel tried to change the subject. "Well, from the way things here have been abandoned, it's not likely these guys will return any time soon. I think something scared the shit out of them." Just then they heard moaning coming from the floor above. Nervously, they all laughed.

"Well," he continued, "I think we're all sleep deprived and tired. We'd better go home and get some rest. We've got a lot of stuff to do tomorrow, and we're not going to get any rest here!"

Chapter 29- Monday Morning

Joel, Jake, and Ariel rose early Monday morning to begin implementing the plan to blow up Project Séance.

First, Ariel called in sick, telling Joanna that she had to take a "mental health week". Then, she called her gynecologist, stating that she needed to get into her office right away, since she had experienced some "excruciating cramping" over the weekend and needed to find out the cause of her discomfort.

Joel and Jake drove to the center, where Joel worked. Joel went inside to see his patient Tunisha. Meanwhile, Jake snuck out behind cars at the center parking lot. He removed a current license plate from one car, then he moved over to the center's patient transportation van, removing those plates. He put the car's plates on the truck and took the van plates with him. He opened the front door by unlocking the passenger door lock with a Slim Jim lockout kit. He inserted the tool in front of the window into the door, unlatching the lock. Once inside the van, he opened the glove box to steal the registration.

Joel explained to the staff he wouldn't be in the office for the next week, but he made it a point to talk with Tunisha for the first time, since she returned from the hospital. She sat down in his office, hanging her head shamefully. She seemed saddened by the thought that she had disappointed Dr. Russell.

"I know what I did was wrong, Doctor Joel," Tunisha stated apologetically. "I didn't mean to be a bother to anyone."

"Listen, Tunisha. I know you are hurting. I also wanted you to know that I read your journals while you were in the hospital."

Joel waited for a response.

"Really?"

"Are you angry? I mean, I really didn't have permission to do so. I just wanted to see what I felt you didn't want to tell me."

"No, I'm not, Doctor Joel. I don't think I could ever be mad at you."

"Do you know what I saw in those journals, Tunisha?"

"No."

"I saw a bright, young girl with a wonderful future ahead of her, whose life was almost cut short. I saw a lot of pain, and it made me sad, Tunisha." Joel waited again, but Tunisha just sat quietly.

"I think you are also very talented, and I think you have great promise as a writer or poet."

"Really, Doctor Joel? You think so?"

"Absolutely. But you know what else I found in those journals?"

Tunisha again became quiet.

"I saw the email from Tony."

Tunisha began to cry.

"Tunisha, I know you feel you loved Tony. I know you felt that he was talking to you. And, I know that you tried to kill yourself, because you wanted to be with him. But let me tell you this: I know for a fact that the person who sent you this email was not your Tony. They were playing a very cruel joke with your feelings."

She held her face in her hands as she cried more audibly.

Dr. Russell got up from his chair and knelt down before her. He looked into her eyes. "Tunisha, I want you to promise me something, okay?"

"Sure, Doctor Joel."

"It doesn't matter what happens to me or anyone else around here. I want *you* to promise me that you'll continue to write your poetry, write in your journals, do well in school, and continue to live a long and happy life, marrying, having children, and living out your life until you die of natural causes at a ripe old age. And I want you to promise me that you won't shut the people who care about you out of your life, just because you're afraid of getting hurt. Do you promise me that you will do that?"

"I'll try, Doctor Joel."

"I know you will, Tunisha. I know you will try your best."

When Joel walked out to the parking lot, Jake reclined in his car, taking a cat nap. He awoke when Joel climbed in the driver's seat.

"Hey, Doc. Okay, we are going to have to buy a Ford Transit Connect Van. Fortunately, it was a cheap one, and it didn't have the Passive Anti-Theft System. Dang, I hope they don't figure I switched these plates for at least a couple of days."

Concerned, Jake asked Joel, "How'd it go?"

"Okay. It went okay." Joel had a sad look about him, and Jake sensed that sadness in the tone of his voice. He felt as if he had just bid farewell to an old friend for the last time. Then Joel turned to Jake. "What next?"

"First we gotta pick up my girl, and then we gotta go buy this van."

It turned out that Ariel wasn't able to meet with her gynecologist that morning. So instead, she reported to the nearest emergency room. She complained of symptoms of severe lower abdominal pain, and she stated that she hadn't had a routine pelvic exam in about three years. The triage nurse showed her into the examination room, handed her a gown, and told her to undress and wait for the physician.

As soon as the nurse left the room, Ariel searched through the cabinets that were unlocked. She found a stack of hospital gowns in varying sizes, and a couple of packaged syringes and needles. Also, someone had left a stethoscope. She shoved all these items into her suspiciously large handbag and snuck out of the hospital, before anyone had noticed her missing.

Later, Joel, Jake, and Ariel all drove to the local Ford dealership to buy a van. Monday morning was typically a slow time for dealerships, so the saleswoman was very happy to help and spend as much time as necessary with the potential buyers. She seemed especially delighted that they knew exactly what model and color cargo van they wanted, and she was elated when she found the van that they wanted was already in their floor plan.

Joel was not a very good liar, but Jake played his role with style. "Daddy is taking me on a road trip." He looked sheepishly at Joel and leaned up to him. "Aren't you, Daddy? I love my Dad. And Sis is going with us." He put his arm around Ariel, pulling her closer to him. "I love my Sis...."

Ariel slapped Jake on the back of the head again. "Stop touching me, you jerk!" she quipped.

Jake shrugged at the saleswoman. "Sisters. You gotta love 'em."

This made the saleswoman a bit uneasy, but she didn't let Jake's strange behavior deter her from making the sale. Joel paid cash for the vehicle and requested that the entire thing be titled in Ariel's name as a gift. After three hours of test drives and pretending to be—as Jake put it—one "super happy family", the sale was finalized, the van was washed and fueled, and the saleswoman waved goodbye as the three deviants drove away.

But, contrary to the story Jake had given the naïve saleswoman, they were not headed on a family road trip. They were headed out to Home Depot to buy, as Jake put it, "a crapload of kerosene."

Chapter 30- Trying to Buy Time

Almost every major strip mall in the Saint Louis metro region had at least one home improvement store—a Home Depot or a Lowe's—or sometimes both. There were a lot of suburbanites trying to engineer a lot of home improvement projects on their own. This worked to Joel and Jake's advantage, because most of their bomb making supplies (aside from the actual explosives) could be bought at one of these stores.

The plan was to purchase eight 5-gallon containers of kerosene. Since only a few were available at each store, they would have to go to at least three. They would simply buy enough kerosene not to draw suspicion, along with other household items and electrical supplies, and then move on to the next store.

Jake, having been homeless for the past year, stopped to fondle every bit of equipment and machinery necessary for home improvement.

"Look, Doc. Cordless weed whackers are on sale! Let's get one!" he cried out to Joel, several aisles down. Then he picked up the hedge trimmer, pretending to start it up and whack weeds. All the while, he mimicked fake motor noises by vibrating his lips.

"They're on sale, because it's December, you dope!" Ariel snatched the hedge trimmer from Jake and placed it back on the shelf. She walked past him, down two aisles to the Christmas section.

"Joel, let's get a Christmas tree. You need something pretty in your house. It's so....masculine." She said the word "masculine" as if it were something she found truly disgusting. "Jake and I will help decorate."

Jake followed her. "Yeah, Doc. Oh, and let's get a big-ass tree—one with lights already on it." Jake pointed to the tallest and most gorgeous pre-lit tree on the display stand. "Only $239, Doc! It's a steal....Look, a spruce.....makes me think of Christmas in New York. Well, you're rich. You can afford it." Jake laughed. "We can load this sucker into the van and have it up in no time."

"Ooooh, let's get some glass ornaments, too. They have color-coordinated ones in big plastic bins. Not as unique as the Hallmark ones, but some pretty ones." Ariel now begged sheepishly.

"Can we get some, Doc?" Jake asked.

Joel found his companions' behavior amusing. He felt almost as though he was a young father, carting his two small toddlers to the toy store. They wanted to buy everything they saw, and they were begging him to buy everything that struck their fancy.

Jake held up a plastic menorah, modeling it like Vannah White. "And Doc, don't forget your Jewish friends out there!" He started to sing the Dreidel song. "Dreidel, dreidel, dreidel, I made you out of clay. Dreidel, dreidel, dreidel...."

Joel seemed entertained by Jake and Ariel and consented to the Christmas purchases. After Jake stopped by the electrical department to get some wiring and necessary bomb making tools, Joel and Jake loaded the already assembled tree into the back of the van. Meanwhile, Ariel hauled out several bags of ornaments, candles, lights, and garland in a shopping cart. As a matter of fact, the originally sought items—the kerosene and electrical supplies— had suddenly taken a back seat to the Christmas impulse buys.

But Joel sensed Ariel and Jake's childlike excitement about their acquired purchases. And, for the first time in eight years, even *he* became giddy with anticipation for the season. He hadn't celebrated Christmas since Elsa died, and it felt as though Jake and Ariel's excitement was fast becoming infectious.

Throughout the afternoon, Joel appreciated the company of his two companions. On several occasions during their afternoon shopping spree, he caught himself laughing out loud, mostly at Jake's silly antics. He also noticed that Ariel had warmed up to Jake throughout the day. Joel was amazed that, despite all that Jake had been through during his lifetime, he never seemed to lose his sense of humor. He possessed an innate ability to diffuse—not only bombs—but other tense situations by making light of them. It almost seemed to Joel that Jake and Ariel might make a suitable couple, since Jake's humor seemed to offset some of Ariel's anxiousness.

After the trio had acquired the last of the kerosene that Jake had calculated they would need, they all boarded the van. Ariel asked to make one last stop.

"Joel, can we stop by the beauty supply shop?" she asked. She ran her fingers through Jake's unruly locks. "I need to get some scissors to cut this mop head! Oh, and maybe a little Nix as a precaution."

Jake smiled. "I'll have you know, little lady—I'm completely critter-free."

Joel laughed out loud once more, and Ariel smiled.

It was late in the evening. Joel, Ariel, and Jake decided to stop for a meal before they headed home with the loaded van.

"Where would you guys like to go? There are several great places on the Hill I haven't been to in a while," Joel offered.

"Waffle House!" Jake demanded. "I want Waffle House!"

Ariel rolled her eyes.

"Okay...I guess it's Waffle House," Joel agreed, reluctantly.

Jake cheered, as they headed off to dinner.

When they arrived, Jake again ordered everything on the menu, along with several cups of hot coffee.

"You're gonna be up all night," Joel warned. "And, at the rate you're eating, you're gonna gain back those thirty pounds you lost in the next couple of days."

Ariel picked at a pecan waffle. "I actually like a man with a little meat on his bones." She obviously referred to Jake, but she gazed down at her waffle.

Jake grinned.

After they all partook of the Waffle House pre-holiday feast, Joel drove Ariel home to her apartment. He and Jake stopped by the brewery to drop off all the kerosene they had purchased. Then, Joel took Jake back to his home. He had made up the living room sofa for Jake to sleep on, as he had done for the previous two nights.

Joel apologized to Jake. "I feel bad for making you sleep on the sofa again, Jake." He fluffed up Jake's pillow. "After all, you're a guest. Maybe *I* should take the sofa tonight."

Jake picked up his blanket and gave Dr. Russell a puzzled look. Even though the sofa was admittedly worn, it was still more pleasant than sleeping on a concrete sidewalk. "No, Doc. You've been good to me. As long as I've known you, you've been good to me. Even after..." He looked down at his feet. "...I mean my own mother doesn't even want me around. I went back to her last year, after I had left the hospital, and she said she was ashamed of me and didn't want to see me again. But, of all people, *you* took me in. I'll never forget that, Doc."

Joel tried to cheer Jake up. "Nonsense. You're not a bother. And frankly, I think our little Ariel might even be taking a shine to you."

"Aw, shucks, Doc. Now you're embarrassing me. I *did* tell you she's the woman of my dreams, didn't I?"

"For real?"

"Yes. I've been dreaming about her for years before you introduced us the other day. She's the woman of my dreams." Jake nestled himself under his covers and thoughtfully put his arms behind his head on the pillow. His position struck Joel as if Jake thought he was reclining for a weekly psychiatric therapy session. "And believe me, Doc. I've had *lots* of dreams about her. Wanna hear?"

"No thanks. I'm afraid it might make me blush." Dr. Russell quickly changed the subject. "So, tell me Jake. When did you first realize you could see into the future?"

"When I was stationed in Kandahar. You know, after the blast. At first, they just patched me up and sent me back out into the field. But then, my commanding officers and all my buddies would get freaked out, so they just kept moving me around from unit to unit until my tour was over."

"What do you mean, when you say you 'freaked them out'?"

"Well, when my buddies would go out on a mission, I would know which ones wouldn't be coming back. I would see them dying in my head. At first, I made the mistake of saying something to them. At times, I would try to intervene or help change things, but my technique always backfired. And when I got that feeling, I was always right. They didn't come back. Finally, the guys were asking me, 'Am I gonna make it back, Jakie?' By that time, even if I got a bad feeling, I would just say 'Hell, yeah, dude!' and brush it off. But you know me, Doc. They could tell just by reading my face that I was lying.

"Anyway, when the news got around to the CO that I knew who wasn't gonna make it, they'd figured out that nobody wanted to go out, if they thought I knew they were gonna die. Pretty soon, *nobody* wanted to go out. So, they'd just ship me off to another unit. Finally, I ended up driving a supply truck until my tour ended. I guess they figured if I could see into the future, I could at least drive a truck of ammo safely to base and get there in one piece.

Of course, by that time, nobody wanted to get to know me or be my buddy anymore. And I realized that people don't wanna know what's gonna happen to them. If they knew how crappy their lives would be, they wouldn't bother to get out of bed in the morning. They'd all be like you and me, just floating through life and waiting for the Grim Reaper to take 'em all home."

Dr. Russell sat down on the edge of the coffee table, silently and intently watching Jake as he spoke.

Jake continued. "They told me, when I was done with my tour, they would give me an honorable discharge. But they also said never to come back—ever." Jake looked at Joel. "You see, Doc. It's *not* that they *didn't* believe me. It's that they *did* believe me. And that scared the shit out of them. It freaked them out. And nobody wants a freak around."

Jake paused. "That's why Ariel and I—we have a lot in common. She's a freak, too. But she hides it better than I do. And it's not perfect. Sometimes we get things wrong, because we don't really understand things yet. But that's because they haven't happened yet. But then, they do and we're like—oh yeah, I guess I can see where *that* came from...."

"What about your father, Jake? Whatever happened to him?" Joel asked.

"He divorced my mother when I was six and remarried. He started a new family and had a couple of kids by her."

"Where is he now? Do you talk to him?"

"No. I used to go visit him during the summers, up until I was about ten. Pretty much, he had his new family to deal with, and he didn't need me hanging around. That's why, when I graduated from high school, I went straight into the service. He's a doctor in Manhattan."

"What kind of a doctor?" Joel inquired.

Jake snickered and looked directly at Joel. "—a psychiatrist."

Joel considered the irony of the Jake's situation for just a brief moment and then snickered along with him. Then, Joel rose and patted Jake on the knee. "Well, I guess you need to catch some zees. We've got a couple of long nights ahead of us. I'm going to check my messages and go to bed. Good night."

"G'night, Doc."

On the way up to his bedroom, Joel checked his voice mail. He had three messages on his cell phone. He punched in his pin code.

Message 1: *Hello, Doctor Russell. This is Emma Stokes from the Ford dealership. I just wanted to thank you for your business again and encourage you to fill out the customer satisfaction survey we will be sending you on Ariel's van. If I haven't earned a five in every category, please give me a call, and I will make it right.*

Joel hit the delete key to get to the second message.

Message 2: *Hey, uh.....Doctor Russell? This is Craig, the landlord at the brewery warehouses. Listen, I don't know what the hell you've got going on upstairs, but I've had a bunch of complaints about the noise from other renters. Some have been scared away. I went there myself this morning, and there's quite a lot of noise going on up there. It's locked, and I can't see what's going on.*

I know I didn't ask too many questions before, but I've got people threatening to call the police. Anyway, you need to call me as soon as you get this message.

Joel hit the save key to save the message.

Message 3: *Joel, it's Joanna. I've been thinking about the other day, and I need to talk to you. It's important, so please call me.*

As Joel hit the 7 key to save Joanna's message, he flopped down on his bed, exhausted. *I'll take care of this in the morning*, he thought to himself. *I need to buy some time.* He yawned. Laying on his back, still fully clothed, Dr. Russell drifted off to sleep.

Joel had recently been feeling reinvigorated, perhaps due to the energizing chaos ensuing in his life. But this morning he awoke with a sense of foreboding. He would have to call Craig, the landlord, to buy some time for him and Jake to plant the bomb in the warehouse. He dreaded calling Craig, but he did manage to dial his number on his cell. He spoke with Craig, who was still terribly upset.

"I don't know. I'm locked out myself! Look, if you give me a couple of days to get in there, I will have all my stuff out by the weekend. Look, what do you want me to do? Blow the place up?...Well, I'm sorry. I can't help that. That's right—the weekend. 'Til then, you will just need to keep everybody out of there. Goddammit, that's the best I can do! Take it or leave it!"

Exasperated, Joel hung up the phone. It if wasn't a cell phone, he probably would have slammed the receiver down into its cradle. *That's technology for you. Nowadays, you can't take out all your frustrations on inanimate objects. Everything breaks too easily.*

Dr. Russell had surprised himself when he considered the sheer number of times he had lost his temper in the last week alone. On the one hand, he seemed to be experiencing emotions and feelings he had long kept at bay. It was as if he had been wearing a raincoat on his emotions since Elsa died. With the disastrous results brought on by Project Séance, he was forced to consider his own feelings about life and death. His recent interactions with Jake and Ariel seemed to exacerbate his latent feelings about love and loneliness.

Dr. Russell made one last call to Joanna Watson's voice mail before descending the steps of his upstairs bedroom. "Hey, Joanna. It's Joel. I did get your message late yesterday. It's 10 A.M. I'll stop by today at lunch. See you in two hours."

Joel hung up his call and went downstairs to find Ariel, with scissors in hand, trimming Jake's hair in the kitchen. Jake straddled the kitchen chair and looked like a new man. He was proudly wearing a new pair of corduroys he had gotten from Old Navy and a new pair of Converse sneakers Joel had bought for him at some athletic shoe store. Jake was also wearing an old, brown argyle sweater. Joel recognized the sweater as his own. Jake looked very preppy.

"Good morning, sleepyhead," Jake greeted. He pulled at the shoulders of his sweater. "Look, I'm Mini-Doc!"

Joel didn't laugh. He was still fuming from the shouting match he had on his cell phone just minutes earlier.

"What's up, Doc?" Jake asked.

"Oh, just pissed. That's all," Joel replied.

"What's going on, Joel?" Ariel further prodded.

"Oh, I just got a call from Craig about the noise at the brew house—and another call from Joanna. I'm sure she wants to make trouble," Joel stated. I have to go see her at lunch."

Maybe you should give her a nooner, Doc. Loosen her up a little," Jake quipped.

Joel sat down at the kitchen table. "You're being unfair, Jake. If she's bitchy to me, I'm sure it's my fault."

"You shouldn't have bedded her down, Doc—being a married man and all. But, good thing is you're not anymore. Maybe you should hook up with her again. She's hot. Do ya love her?" Jake asked.

"—Wait a minute," Ariel interrupted. "Joel, you mean—you and Joanna—while Elsa was alive?"

Jake turned to look at Ariel. "Yeah, didn't you know that stuff was going on? How special are your freak powers anyway?" Then, when Jake realized Ariel wasn't aware of Joel's affair with Joanna, donned a more serious expression. "You mean, you really didn't know?"

Joel hesitated to answer Ariel, who looked devastated. Despite her gifted insight into people and situations, this discovery took her completely by surprise. She had never suspected Joel capable of any sort of deception toward Elsa, much less of an affair with Joanna.

Realizing he had opened a Pandora's box, Jake tried to backpedal by trying to console Joel. "It's okay, Doc. We're all human. Plus, it takes two to tango—especially the horizontal tango."

"Well, I called it off before Elsa died, and I'm afraid Joanna's still embittered about it. I don't blame her. I treated her horribly."

Then Joel quickly changed his tone from one of regret to one of decisiveness. "Anyway, I need to go down, smooth things over, and buy us some time. I guess you guys can just hang here today. We'll need to get going once it gets dark. Meanwhile, you guys can empty the Christmas stuff out of the van so we have room for explosives. I'll grab some groceries for dinner and make lots of coffee. It's going to be a long night."

"Don't worry about us, Doc." Jake winked at Ariel. "We'll find something to do. Hey, Doc. Maybe leave us your credit card?"

Joel handed Jake his credit card. "You guys are just hanging with me for my money, aren't you?"

"No, Doc," Jake answered. "We love you *in spite* of your money."

Ariel grinned, saying nothing. She walked over to Joel, bidding him goodbye with a forgiving hug. "No, Joel. We love you for you. We'll be fine. You have a good day."

Joel had worried about how disclosing the truth about his affair with Joanna to Ariel would affect her opinion of him. He felt guilty as he watched her face—that crushed look of disappointment after discovering that he was only human. He seemed hopeful, however, that she might not actually *hate* him for betraying Elsa.

But he had also hurt Joanna very deeply, and he wasn't sure if *Joanna* didn't hate him. Ariel had never really liked Joanna, but perhaps now she could understand that she wasn't really as cold and selfish as others might perceive her to be. Like everyone else—including Joel—she was only human.

Still, Joel dreaded having to meet with Joanna. He was fairly sure that, based on the way she left his home the other day, she was still pretty pissed. Like most of the people in Dr. Russell's profession, Joanna was a skeptic, and it wasn't likely that she would buy the truth about Project Séance. She knew the project was Joel's brainchild and that it had destroyed lives. But Joanna had guessed that Joel's intentions were more malicious than they actually were. Up to this point in time, he had even tried to destroy the project twice himself, but with no luck.

Joanna was somehow convinced that Joel and Jake were in cahoots the entire time, but the truth was that they had not seen each other at all until the previous weekend. They were not fellow conspirators. And *neither* of them had ever *planned* for Elsa to die. But Joel was not sure that he could convince Joanna of that truth. In fact, he was pretty sure that she would *never* buy the truth.

Dr. Russell's best approach in dealing with Joanna was to charm her. By appealing to her in this manner, he could possibly buy two more days in order to effectively destroy the project. True, if he blew the warehouse up, he would have to answer for the destruction of private property. But at least, if he and Jake followed through with the plan correctly, he wouldn't be responsible for the project's destruction of any more lives.

Joel arrived at his old Chesterfield office promptly at noon. He was no longer the unkempt, confused old man whom Joanna had called into her office a year ago, when she cleaned out his desk and gave him his walking papers. Since he had returned to work at the center, Joel had cleaned himself up. He was cleanly shaven and professionally dressed in a dark pair of trousers and crisp, cotton shirt and modern tie. He wore a long, dark woolen coat. Since he had updated his attire, he had also cut his unruly gray hair. It was still a bit long, but still short enough to keep his wavy locks looking well-groomed and at bay. He somewhat resembled a dashing Einstein without the mustache.

Because Ariel had taken the week off, the receptionist's counter was unoccupied. Joel walked past the counter through the hallway to Joanna's open office door.

She stood from behind her desk and greeted him. "Hello, Joel." and motioned for him to be seated in front of her desk. Everyone else was out to lunch, but she walked over to close her office door just the same. She started to walk back behind her desk to seat herself once again.

Joel stood quickly and grabbed both her hands, seating her instead on the chair next to his in front of the desk. He had decided that he wasn't going to let her hide behind the "desk of power" today. And when he grabbed her hands, he noticed that she suddenly seemed weak. He had also noticed that she seemed as though she hadn't gotten a lot of sleep since their encounter three days before.

"Sit here next to me, Joanna. Let's talk." Joel was surprised that, as much as he dreaded coming to see her, he still felt unexpectedly comfortable around her. It was almost as if it were like the old days, when they were romantically involved. He seemed to be in charge once again, and it was not like their relationship of the past eight years when he always seemed on the defensive. As a matter of fact—at that moment—it was as if they hadn't experienced the last eight years at all. It was almost as if none of that misery had ever occurred.

As Joanna sat down next to Joel, her demeanor changed. Joel believed that, when he had initially arrived, she had hoped to have the upper hand in the conversation. But by moving her out from behind the desk, she was once again vulnerable to him and his undeniable charms. He pushed the two chairs closer together.

Joel knew that, in spite of Joanna's attempts to give him the impression that she had moved on, she was still trapped in his spell. Everything she had done in her career over the past eight years seemed purposeful. Personally, she kept others in her life at an arm's distance. But the truth of the matter was that she, like Joel, was in an emotional limbo. Unlike Joel, she immersed herself in her work to avoid confronting her feelings. Joel, on the other hand, simply tried to avoid feeling altogether.

"Well," she explained, "Joel, I don't know what to do. I have been thinking about the papers I read at your place—about Jake and Elsa—and now Ariel. I know she thinks I hate her, but I don't. I just don't know how to—" Joanna choked.

As they sat next to each other, Joel hugged Joanna to his chest. He spoke softly. "Joanna, I know you don't believe me about this project and about Jake. I don't blame you, either. And I know why you called me here. But you don't have to explain yourself or what you are about to do. I understand that you are doing what you have to. I am only going to ask one thing of you."

Joanna looked up. "What is that?" she asked.

"I'm just asking that you remember what you and I once had together. I'm just asking that you give me three days to make this right."

He placed his hand under her chin and looked deeply into her ice blue eyes. "Joanna, don't you think you know me? I'm still the same man you fell in love with ten years ago. Do you really think I would try to hurt anyone? Surely, you have been doing this job long enough to have me figured out.

"I loved Elsa. Why would I ever want to hurt her? And *you* packed up the tapes of Jake's sessions. You know he threatened me. You know I have never been personally involved with a patient. Why would I lie to you? This whole experiment has just been one horrible fiasco for me. And I need you to give me the chance to make it right. Just give me a few more days. That's all I'm asking."

Joel continued. "Joanna, I'm so very sorry. I feel that I have ruined your life. I may be able to fix this situation with the project, but I don't know how to fix your life. It's true that I told you that I loved only Elsa when I broke it off with you. But the truth is that I also—" Joel stopped for a moment. Then, he drew Joanna's face to his and kissed her.

Joel had not kissed a woman since Joanna kissed him in the men's room the night of Elsa's death eight years ago. He wasn't sure how long it had been since

Joanna kissed a man, but by the way she responded to him, he thought it might have been almost as long for her. Soon, they kissed passionately and fiercely, and Joel had pulled her body closer and tighter to him. On the one hand, they were embracing as if they hadn't known each other in eight years. But on the other hand, they felt as sexually comfortable with each other as if they had just known each other the day before.

Joel stood and reached his hands around either side of Joanna's hips, guiding her off the chair. With one swoop of his right arm, he swept all the files off the corner of Joanna's desk. Then, he perched her there, seated in front of him.

She wore a very becoming blue iris sheath dress. Even though it was winter, she wasn't wearing stockings. *She hardly ever wore stockings.* He reached under her skirt and spread her supple thighs as she sighed heavily. Then, he reached under her buttocks and quickly pulled her panties down her legs. He pulled her hips close to him as he stood in front of her, looking straight into her face.

He rubbed his pelvis against hers, and they resumed their impassioned kiss.

Joel's desire for Joanna had now been reawaked after an eight year slumber. He was now fifty-six, but he spontaneously acted like a teenage boy preoccupied with sex. He clumsily unfastened his belt and unzipped his trousers, and Joanna guided his pants down beneath his buttocks. Then, she guided his very erect penis directly into her.

Joel was secretly amazed that, not only had he the desire to still have sex at fifty-six, this time he performed like he was twenty. At most, Joel probably lasted a full minute of ramming Joanna up against the desk. Since it had been so long since he had relations with her, it didn't take long for him to reach a violent, and very long-awaited orgasm.

Without much dialogue at all, Joel and Joanna seemed to have rekindled their relationship. And in their haste to do so, they didn't have time to reminisce about old times or even remove any major bit of clothing to prolong the moment. They were behaving almost like animals during the mating season. And they had held it off for so long and wanted it for so long that the final result was one long minute of passionate, heated bliss.

Ironically, Joel didn't take Jake's comment about the "nooner" seriously. But in reality, that's exactly what he had—a very long overdue nooner. And ultimately, they were both fortunate that the entire office was empty, because—even with the door closed—their very audible groans of pleasure would most certainly have been heard down the hallway.

Reeling from his climax, Joel hid his face in Joanna's breast to catch his breath. He thought to himself for a moment. *Why can't Joanna and I have a life together? Haven't I been punishing myself long enough? Haven't we both been punishing ourselves long enough?*

Then he looked up at Joanna and kissed her one long time, holding her face in his hands. "I have to go." He hurriedly fastened his pants and his belt and grabbed his wool coat, kissing her again while she was still perched on the desk. "I'm just asking for three more days, Joanna. That's all I need. I will make this right. I promise."

Joanna nodded in agreement, speechless. She was still perched on the desk as Joel ran out, slamming the door behind him. She pushed herself off the edge of her massive desk and turned to examine the files, which had been whisked to the floor moments earlier. It was as if a human tornado had cut through the building and had taken with him every feeling of bitterness and resentment she had coddled for the last eight years. All it left in its wake was a woman, unequivocally disheveled and in shock, standing over a stack of patient files in heaps on the floor.

Chapter 32- Dance Me to the End of Love

Joel returned to his home in Dogtown with two paper bags full of groceries, a brand new coffeemaker, and a bottle of wine. When he arrived, he discovered that Ariel and Jake had assembled their newly purchased Christmas tree and decorated it. In addition, they had ignited a fire with a Dura Log stoked in his small living room fireplace. Ariel had strategically placed some of the few candles and decorations they had acquired the day before throughout the downstairs. She even unpacked Joel's box of belongings and pictures, placing them carefully on the fireplace mantle and coffee table. The smells of a wood burning fire and evergreen permeated Joel's home.

He sniffed the air. "Hello? Do I smell evergreen?"

"Yeah, Doc," Jake answered. "Straight from the can!" He lifted up a can of fake evergreen scent they had purchased at the dollar store earlier that afternoon.

Ariel had lit a few of the Christmas candles on the coffee table. They also had some Christmas music playing through the small speakers attached to Joel's computer workstation.

"We tried to make this place something you'd like to come home to. You know, something in keeping with the season," Ariel commented.

"You like?" Jake quizzed. "Hey, Doc. Guess what you bought me for Christmas with your credit card— an ipod! Isn't this awesome? I've never owned an ipod."

"Me neither," responded Joel.

"No, really. I already downloaded 500 songs on itunes today. Oh, by the way, you have an itunes account now, Doc." Jake mentioned this all to Joel very matter-of-factly.

"Five hundred songs?" Joel was astonished. "Isn't that a bit pricey? What, aren't they like a buck a piece?"

"Well," Jake hesitated. "Some are actually $1.29, but if you buy the album, they're usually about $10.00. Yeah, I know what you're thinking, Doc. But you didn't have one CD around here. Christ, you don't even have a fuckin' TV! Plus, I don't feel right about stealing songs over the internet. That would be stealing someone's livelihood."

"But stealing my money to pay for the songs on the internet is okay?" Joel had a tone of sarcasm in his voice, but Jake could tell that he was only teasing.

"No, Doc. This is stuff that you will like. Well, us too. We like it, but you will, too. Look...I've got Bob Marley, Pink Floyd, Nirvana..."

"—and Christmas music," Ariel added.

"Yeah, Christmas music, too." Jake clicked around the computer playlist using the computer mouse to play bits of songs that he purchased and downloaded. He was only playing short segments, before he moved on to the next great song to play. It was like he was an old K-tel record commercial. Of course, Joel only thought that to himself. He wouldn't bother wasting his time trying to tell this joke to two young kids who probably never owned a vinyl record in their lives.

"Listen, Joel," Ariel walked over to the computer and selected a song, picking one from a list of Leonard Cohen songs she had downloaded. She chose *Dance Me to the End of Love*.

"Didn't you and Elsa like Leonard? He had a concert here last year. I wanted to go so badly, but the tickets were sky high. This one makes me think of the two of you, when you were together."

Reminiscing, Joel smiled and pursed his lips. As the music began playing, he was suddenly drawn into the swaying rhythms of the bass and brush drums. The female background singers descanted their haunting "la la las", accompanied by the spooky chords of what was possibly a Hammond organ. He recalled dancing to this song with Elsa in the music room at the old estate and was suddenly taken back in time. This newer version that Ariel played was more recent than the one Joel and Elsa danced to. The singer's voice had aged a bit over the last quarter century. It was much raspier than Joel remembered. And Mr. Cohen's range was significantly lower than it was when he was younger. But this was still unmistakably Leonard Cohen's voice.

As the singer began the first verse, Joel set his groceries down on the kitchen counter and stepped back into the living room. He walked toward Ariel, stretching out his arm to invite her to dance. "You should have called me to take you to the concert, little Ariel. I would have taken you as my date. May I?"

Ariel nodded, but apologized first. "I don't really know how to ballroom dance, Joel."

"I taught Elsa to dance. I can teach you. He reached his arm around Ariel's waist. I believe this song is a slow foxtrot, if I remember correctly. So, grab my left hand, and I will lead."

During the musical interludes, Joel was touched by the music. The small computer speakers were playing this live version of the song so clearly that he could almost see the clarinetist and guitarist playing their solos in the room. As the music continued, Joel was moved by the trills and runs of the solo clarinet and the feverish manner in which the guitarist plucked out his musical responses to the singer's words.

"The first two steps are slow, and the last two steps are quick. So, you begin by stepping back on your right foot first. Slow, slow, then right to the side—quick, quick."

Ariel tried to follow as Joel led. She glanced down, concentrating on her feet.

"Don't look down at your feet," he corrected. "Look at me. Wait. Stop. Breathe. Now, feel the music as you move with me."

Joel was now the dance instructor, instructing Ariel on the complexities of ballroom dance. Jake sat the dance out, watching Joel and Ariel try to navigate the small living room of his Dogtown house. They maneuvered around the coffee table, newly erected Christmas tree, and the maze of decorations. All the while, Ariel inadvertently enchanted Jake with her beauty. During brief moments, Joel would catch a glimpse of Jake goggling at Ariel. As transparent as Jake was, Joel could see that Jake was both fascinated by her and also infatuated with her.

Ariel picked up the steps that Joel taught her with speed and ease now. They had progressed through the promenade and had now added a few turns. She seemed to be enjoying her dance lessons while appreciating her partner's advanced skills. She knew that Joel imagined himself dancing with Elsa, but Ariel didn't mind standing in on her friend's behalf.

During the lessons, Joel also enjoyed dancing with Ariel. Here he was, dancing in the company of a beautiful young woman, once again feeling alive. These days he spent with Ariel and Jake were the highlight of the latter part of the most miserable years of his life. When he had lost Elsa, he had lost everything. Yet, he found himself at last in the company of people who cared about him, who wanted to help him, and who needed him.

As Joel turned Ariel and the clarinet played its gypsy interlude between verses, Joel thought of the lyrics being sung. He contemplated the rekindled flame with Joanna, which he had long thought was extinguished. He was surprised to think that, perhaps, he did have room in his life for Joanna.

But mostly at this moment, dancing to the dance he once shared with Elsa, Joel became very hopeful— hopeful about his life and possible future love with Joanna. And he was hopeful about the companion- ship he had shared with Jake and Ariel in recent days. *If I could only move past this point where I have to overcome this nightmare consuming me now, I would be okay,* Joel thought to himself.

All these intense feelings had flooded Joel during the three repeats of the song. As the song ended for the last time, Joel led Ariel into a final turn.

But this time, he had accidentally turned her too close to the coffee table, and she knocked his and Elsa's wedding photo onto the floor, shattering the frame as it fell.

They stopped dancing.

Ariel looked down in horror. "Oh, shit!" She picked up the photo and tried to retrieve the broken bits of glass as she knelt there. "I'm sorry, Joel. I broke..." As she studied the damaged wedding photo remembering Elsa, she wept.

Joel knelt down beside her and put his arm around her shoulder to comfort her. "It's okay," he assured her. As he tried to console her about the loss which he previously and errantly believed was his alone, he realized that losing Elsa was hard on *everyone*, not just him. He spoke to Ariel calmly. "The day Elsa died, a piece of everyone who ever cared for her died with her. I realize that now. And I'm sorry, kiddo. I'm sorry I wasn't there for you."

Jake sat apart, first watching Joel and Ariel as they danced and then watching Joel as he consoled her. For the first time ever, he stood silently. He knew there wasn't anything he could do or say to either of them to take away the years of pain he had caused.

Then, Jake decided he would try to lighten the mood by playing another selection on the computer. This time, Jake chose to play a Bonnie Raitt song entitled, *Dimming of the Day*. He approached Ariel, still tearful and kneeling next to Joel in front of the broken picture.

"May I, m'lady? I don't dance as well as Doc, but I can't pass up a good Bonnie Raitt song." Jake smiled and held out his hand.

Joel gave Ariel an encouraging nod. "You two dance. I'm going to make dinner."

Jake pulled Ariel close to him, and she wrapped her arms high around his neck to move in. As Joel rose to walk to the kitchen, he watched Jake rub his cheek against Ariel's. Her back was to Joel, but he could see Jake wink at him and give him the secret "okay" sign behind her waist.

"I saw that, Jake!" Ariel snapped. She reached behind her back, grabbed his hand, and wrapped it around her waist again.

Joel smiled, shrugged his shoulders, and made his way to the kitchen to cook dinner for the dancing couple. As he unboxed and hooked up the new coffee pot, he overheard Jake singing the lyrics to the Bonnie Raitt song in Ariel's ear.

The day was, indeed, dimming. Joel had soon prepared dinner and invited the dancing couple to partake in the meal—the first meal he had prepared for anyone but himself in his home since Elsa's death. He decided that he actually enjoyed preparing dinner, visiting with his company, and discussing the topics of their pleasant conversation.

As usual, Jake ate everything on his plate. Then he ate everything left on Ariel's plate. Referring jokingly to Joel's culinary skills, he stated, "Great grub, Doc. You're gonna make some guy a lucky man one day!"

Joel chuckled. "Thanks, Jake." He paused for a moment and then heaved out a great sigh of dread. "Well, I suppose we need to get going. Are you guys ready? Jake, bring the thermos!"

And with that, they headed out the door to begin their night's errands.

Chapter 33- The Illegal Acquisition of Combustibles

Joel had purchased a white, Ford Transit cargo van. Although a passenger van was being used to transport patients at the center to and from certain off-campus activities, this was a cargo van. The windows from the side were occluded, and there was limited ability to see through the back windows. They had no shelving installed, in order to make room for the many bags of ammonium nitrate explosives they had hoped to acquire. There was a partition between the cargo hold in the back and the two front seats.

The drive from Dogtown to Southwestern Illinois was not particularly long, but Ariel had brought Jake's ipod so they could listen to music and make the driving time go by faster. She sat in the passenger's seat, plugging the USB cable into the dash.

"Thanks for getting me a van with Sync, Daddy," she joked. "Now we can play the songs you bought on Jake's ipod."

Jake was riding in the back, chuckling. "Yeah, thanks, Dad."

Ariel was going to play deejay. "You'll like this one, Joel." She selected Adele's *Someone Like You*. "I remember the day you played this in the studio. I thought you might like it. I bought two albums of hers."

"I do like it," Joel commented. "Turn it up."

"Have you seen this chick, Doc?" Jake asked. Then he instructed, "Ariel, show him the album cover on the ipod."

Ariel showed Joel the tiny picture on the ipod screen of Adele's album cover. With his aging eyesight, he struggled to get a good look while continuing to drive down the road.

"She's beautiful," Joel acknowledged. "She reminds me of a babysitter I had in Connecticut, where I grew up. I think I was thirteen. I had a major crush on her." Like Joel's sitter, Adele looked almost as if she had stepped out of 1968. Joel fondly recalled how her false lashes and thick eyeliner made her eyes particularly dramatic. And Adele, like his sitter, also had a dimpled chin.

"Huh," Joel said to himself, puzzled. "That's the first memory I've had of my life before Elsa in a long time."

"She sings like Janice Joplin, but she's way hotter," Jake commented.

"Really? How old is she?" Joel inquired.

"Twenty-three," Ariel answered.

"Too young for me," Jake added. "She's just a baby. Ariel's more *my* age. But Doc likes 'em young. Maybe *you* should call her, Doc!"

After the song ended, Ariel instructed Joel on how to issue voice commands over the Sync system. He was actually getting quite good at calling up tunes. She and Jake had done an outstanding job of guessing what kind of music he might enjoy hearing on the ipod and bought an entire library of songs for him. Occasionally, the system would fail to pick up a voice command or find a song. And rarely, it would completely misinterpret a voice command. Then Joel would curse, and Ariel and Jake would laugh. Eventually, they would manage to make another successful selection.

"Play artist Pink Floyd," Jake commanded.

With that, the Sync system played *Another Brick in the Wall*, followed by the song *Money*.

Driving down the road, listening to music he hadn't heard in years, Joel realized how much he missed having music in his life. As he listened to some of the songs which had been popular during his youth, he thought—not only of his life with Elsa—but also of his life *before* Elsa. When she died, Joel thought that somehow the music in his life had died with her. Perhaps that was why he had discarded all his old records and CDs. Maybe that was why he didn't allow himself to play and keep Lillian's piano.

Dr. Russell had often recommended music therapy to many of his patients, particularly those who were troubled by auditory hallucinations or tinnitus. Music had a soothing quality for those who suffered from mood disorders. Also, for the more psychotic patients, it often served to drown out extraneous noises and calm disordered thinking patterns. Sometimes, it kept his patients more in tune with the here and now, if the patient had suffered from a break with reality. Conversely, sometimes it would stir up violence or a traumatic flashback. That sort of a response was not always desirable, but it still might be therapeutic, nonetheless.

Ariel and Jake, like Joel, were musicians. And, like Joel, they were also somewhat troubled individuals. They understood the need for creative people to have a creative outlet for their emotions, especially if they were stuck performing particularly menial tasks throughout the day. Music was essential for most humans to soothe anxiety, to motivate, and to enable recall of latent memories and emotions. Somehow, Jake and Ariel perceptively determined that Joel needed a little more music in his life in order to simply begin feeling more alive.

"Thanks for giving me your ipod, Jake. I really like the songs you guys picked," Joel had stated, commandeering ownership of the electronic device.

"Sure, Doc. Hey, wait. You are gonna buy me my own, aren't you?" Jake asked.

"Sure. We should all have ipods. Everybody gets an ipod!" Joel cried happily.

Once the three had taken the highway from Saint Louis and crossed over the Mississippi River into

Southwestern Illinois, they stopped at the first available rest stop in order to change into their costumes. Joel had never been a good liar, so the plan was that he would dress in normal clothes, wear his State of Missouri ID badge, and simply pretend to be himself.

Ariel had donned a pair of blue surgical scrubs and Raminder's lab coat. Being much more petite than Raminder, she rolled up the sleeves, placed some first aid tape over the photo on the back of his badge, and then attached that to her lab coat.

Jake had traded in all his street clothes for one of the hospital gowns that Ariel had swiped from the hospital emergency room earlier that day. He gave Ariel a stun gun to use in case of an emergency.

"Where did you get this?" Joel asked, referring to the stun gun.

"Uh, you don't really want to know. But it may come in handy," Jake answered.

Jake had the locations of several active coal mines and quarries mapped out as potential destinations. He planned to acquire at least fifty 50-pound bags of ammonium nitrate prills, along with blasting caps, Tovex sausage, and any other useful explosive devices they might find. With fifty bags in tow, Jake calculated, they would mix the prills with the forty gallons of kerosene they had acquired on Monday. They would go down the list of coal mines and quarries, which were ordered by the least guarded and most convenient down to the most secure and most impenetrable.

Although Southwestern Illinois and Southeastern Missouri were dotted with many abandoned coal mines, there were a few coal mines still operational, more of the active ones being located in Illinois. Plus, there were many aggregate and stone quarries throughout the region.

It was now Tuesday night, and the sky was dark. Their first stop was a coal mine, which was being mined 24/7, but the majority of the workers were underground at that time of night. The locked shed contained the mine's explosives, located above ground. The shed was also not guarded. The three thieves managed to park in the darkness off the side of an adjoining road, which was obscured by trees. The trek from the van was about 500 feet, but they could steal the contents of the shed virtually undetected. Unfortunately, they would have to lug as many heavy bags as they could through the heavily wooded area back to the van.

They snuck out behind the padlocked shed, and Jake broke the lock. "Dang, that was easy," he surprisedly whispered. The shed was not particularly well lit. But the almost full moon illuminated the mine's storage shed enough to enable them to move what contents they could find without being detected. "There's a pretty good amount of shit in here, Doc. I'd say about twenty-five bags of nitro. And, look! Here are all the blasting caps we need! Oooh, here's even some sausage." Jake was like a kid in a candy store.

Despite how out of shape he had become since his time in the service, Jake was still able to haul two 50-pound bags on his back through the woods easily. Joel and Ariel could haul one bag each. Silently, but steadily, they were able to move the twenty-five 50-pound bags within seven or eight return trips. They lined the bags up side by side in a five-by-five arrangement along the length of the floor of the van in order to evenly distribute the weight. Jake traveled in the back of the van sitting atop the illegally acquired bags, while Ariel sat in the passenger's seat and Joel drove.

The next stop they made was to a small quarry nearby. It wasn't secure, but they didn't acquire as many explosives as they had hoped. This time, there only seemed to be about five bags of ammonium nitrate in total. It was now midnight and Jake used the second set of bags as a seat.

Heading northward on highway 255, Joel found himself getting sleepy during the drive. Although he tried to play some more upbeat songs on the ipod to keep himself awake, his driving veered between lanes of the road ever so slightly. A police car, which had been sitting in the darkness, flashed its siren and approached them from behind, pulling them off to the shoulder.

"Uh, guys, it's show time," Jake commented from the back.

Ariel turned off the music.

The police officer approached Joel's window, as he opened it. "Good evening, officer," he greeted.

"Yes, sir. I noticed you were swerving a bit on the highway."

"Yes, officer. I was a bit distracted." Joel bit his lip, and pointed to Jake in the back, who was perched behind the cargo window, making a terrible racket and acting like a lunatic.

"Could I have your driver's license and registration, please? Ariel pulled the stolen registration from the glove compartment and Joel gave the police office his driver's license.

"Here's my State of Missouri I.D. as well," Joel offered.

"Exactly what is your business here, Doctor Russell?"

"I am a psychiatrist. This guy in the back is an escaped mental patient. I am transporting him back to Saint Louis."

By this time, Jake was making cackling noises and barking like a dog.

"And this is," the officer flashed his flashlight on Ariel's badge. "Doctor Singh?" He looked a bit puzzled. "I didn't think psychiatrists made deliveries."

"Well, this particular gentleman has been a patient of mine for eight years, so I know him quite well," Joel assured.

"We're used to it, officer. We do this kind of thing a lot," she replied. She turned back, addressing Jake. "Hey, quiet down back there, or I'm gonna have to Taser your ass!"

The officer looked a bit disturbed. "Is he violent?"

"No," Joel replied. He's virtually harmless. He's just—" Joel attempted to make "crazy" loops with his index finger so that Jake couldn't see. He turned to Ariel and said, "Why don't you get a sedative ready for him, just in case we need to use it."

Ariel nodded and pulled out a syringe, pretending to aspirate a drug into her syringe. Of course, it was nothing more than isotonic saline, but the officer didn't know that. "Quiet down back there, or we're gonna have to put you down!" She turned to the officer. "He just needs a little tough love," she sneered.

The officer detected the smell of ammonia emanating from the back. By this time, Jake had quieted down. Ariel noticed him sniffing for the explosives in back and volunteered, "Yeah, he likes to soil himself. It's a mess back there. Don't sniff too hard. You're welcome to take a look," she offered. "But I'll warn you. He likes to smear his poop all over everything, and he might hit you with a turd, if you open that back door." Jake laughed, almost demonically.

The officer looked disgusted and shook his head. "No thanks. I'll pass." He handed Joel's identification back to him, along with the stolen registration. "Just drive more carefully, will you? Good luck, Doctor."

The State Trooper moved back to get in his car, parked behind their van. As he got back in, Jake mooned him, smashing his bare buttocks, which were clearly visible through the back of his hospital gown, against the back window. Then he turned around and made a face saying, "Come and get me, copper!"

At first, the officer looked as if he wanted to call the radio dispatcher. Joel and Ariel held their breath. Then, annoyed, the confused officer shook his head and finally got back into his vehicle and drove away.

Joel took a deep breath of release. "I hate lying," he confided.

"Well, really Doc, you didn't lie at all," Jake assured him. "I *am* an escaped mental patient, and you *are* who you say you are. And, you *are* taking me back to Saint Louis. Well, eventually you are. But, first we gotta get more ANFO and fuel. " Then Jake looked at Ariel, "Little lady, you are quite the actress. But I think you're having a little too much fun with that stun gun."

The final quarry they visited for supplies was located a little closer to the city. It was now 3 A.M., and the quarry was not mining at this time of night. After initially locating and disabling the few security cameras in place, Jake was able to locate twenty more bags of explosives, along with some extra pipes, blasting caps, and supplies he might be able to use. This storage shed was a little bit more easily accessible, and they managed to lay down another layer of the 50 pound bags on top of the initial layer. The van was currently carrying over 3,000 pounds of additional load, but it was fairly evenly distributed about the cargo area to prevent the van from leaning.

Ariel crept around the back to pee behind a building, while Joel and Jake had loaded the last of the bags and blasting supplies in the van. Suddenly, a lone security guard came out to investigate. They were certain, as they noticed the sleepiness in his eyes, that he was abruptly jerked awake from his nightly nap. He confronted Joel and Jake, pointing his gun at them. "Freeze!" he demanded.

Joel and Jake raised their hands. "Aw man, you aren't gonna shoot us, are you dude?" Jake asked.

"If I have to I will! Now stay put!" he demanded. He transferred his pistol to his left hand and picked up the radio transmitter hanging from his belt. Immediately, his eyes widened, as he dropped both his phone and pistol and went into convulsions, falling to the ground. Ariel stood behind him, holding the stun gun. She had zapped the man in the back of the neck. She seemed pleasantly surprised by the overall effectiveness of her weapon, as she stared down at the guard, who was evidently paralyzed.

"Damn, girl," Jake said. "I think you're having way too much fun with that thing!"

Jake grabbed the gun from her. "Here. I'll take that. Now, let's get out of here before he starts moving." They loaded themselves into the van and headed out quickly.

Jake, riding in the back once again, teased, "Ariel loves me, she saved my life." He soon sang his declaration of love. "Ariel loves me.....I love you, too, Ariel!"

"Shut up, Jake," she screamed.

"I love you, too Ariel. Thanks, kiddo." Joel patted her head. "We've got to unload this crap before they catch up with us."

By the time the trio of criminals returned to the brewery, it was 5 A.M. They had very little time to unload the acquisitions of the night, but it was not going to take nearly as long as it had for them to acquire the load. First, they had the advantage of being able to park behind the brew house, obscured from the road. In addition, they could load their supplies onto dollies and pallet hand trucks, transporting them up the freight elevator at the back of the building in virtually no time. However, by the time they unloaded all their supplies into Ariel's small practice room for storage, there was no room in which to walk around. They dismantled all the band equipment and loaded that all into the van, making room for the next night's bomb preparation.

With their truck now filled with band equipment and the band room on the second floor now filled with explosives, Ariel locked the practice room door. Ariel and Jake changed out of their costumes and back into regular street clothes, and they headed back to Joel's Dogtown home to rest.

That morning, Jake had confiscated Aaron's humbucker guitar and serenaded Ariel, while she sat on the living room sofa and sang with him. He strummed as loudly as he could, but he was barely audible because his guitar wasn't plugged into an amplifier.

As Jake played the guitar and Ariel sang, Joel decided to check his email. But as he reviewed the items in his inbox, his heart jolted suddenly, when he realized he had received an incoming email from Timothy_McVeigh06112011@projectseance.com. Secretly, he opened it to read it, trying not to let Ariel and Jake peek at the message.

Attention, Dr. Joel Russell, you self-righteous liberal shrink. Deliver this message to Jake Sternen.

Sergeant Sternen,

I heard what you said about me, calling me a baby killer and a hack.

I would think that you, of all people, would understand what it meant to serve your country, only to find out that the country you had served and loved so well had abandoned your loyalty and the Constitution penned by its forefathers for principles embraced by a bunch of liberal thugs.

Sure, some innocent people had to die for these politicians to take notice, but it's not like they didn't murder innocent women and children in Waco. It if weren't for me, they would still not think twice about the consequences of bullying their free citizens. I was the one who made them stop to realize that they weren't invincible.

Of course, the diatribe went on, so Joel skimmed through before he would be noticed.

As for "breaking my skull" with your bare fists, I can only say this. Bring it on, you Jew pussy!

But you gotta come get me first.

Timothy_McVeigh06112011@projectseance.com

Jake ceased his serenade as Ariel walked to the kitchen to pour herself a glass of orange juice. He stepped behind Joel, who was still reading the computer monitor.

"What ya doin', Doc?" Jake had noticed Joel reading his email. In a moment, Dr. Russell hit his delete button and immediately emptied the email out of his trash bin. He didn't want to mention anything about this email to Jake, for fear it would only serve to provoke him.

"I am about to email Elsa," he informed Jake. "I'm going to see if she will help me." He opened Elsa's email address from the previous week and hit reply, typing his message:

My Dearest Elsa,

If it is really you who sent me this message, then you already understand what horrific things this experiment has caused to happen. If you truly know and love me, then you know what I must do. You will help me destroy this project before it hurts any other innocent people.

Project Séance has done nothing more than to hurt those around me, and since I am the one who brought this thing to fruition, then I am the one who must destroy it. I had hoped I might be able to communicate with you.

I had hoped that, perhaps, I might be able to find closure from losing you so suddenly. But this has just turned into one complete nightmare.

Please help me do this, Elsa. I have always loved you. If you are truly my beloved Elsa, you will do all that you can to help me do the right thing.

Your Devoted Husband,

Joel

"Aw, that's sweet, Doc," Jake commented.

"Yeah, right," Joel answered, simultaneously hitting the send button.

"No, I mean it, Doc." Then, Jake suddenly became pensive and sat down next to Joel. Joel could plainly read that Jake now struggled with his overwhelming feelings of guilt. "You really loved her, didn't you, Doc?"

"Yes, Jake. I did. I wanted so badly to get the chance to talk to her before she died. There was so much left undone, so much to apologize for...." Joel choked on his words.

Jake stifled his tears of regret. "Look, Doc. I don't know how to say this. I know I'm long overdue. I'm really.....sorry. I didn't mean....."

Joel raised his hand to stop Jake. "I know you didn't, Jake. I know you're sorry. I'm sorry, too."

Jake looked blankly down at his feet. Then he looked up at Joel and continued, "No, Doc. I've got to say this. I've ruined everybody's life! I thought I was doing the right thing. I knew you were going to open the gates to hell. I had seen that so very clearly in my dreams. As soon as I got out of the Service and moved here to Saint Louis, I started to have these dreams. It's like—no matter what I did, I couldn't stop them! I couldn't sleep without seeing the scenes replayed in my head over and over again. I saw this huge blast. I saw demons. And I saw your face and heard God's voice tell me your name.

"After I met you, I really didn't want to try to kill you, because I liked you. But who can argue with God? I genuinely believed he sent me on this mission and that I was doing what God wanted me to do. I believed that that's why He let me live, when my buddies..." Jake was clearly tormented, and tears welled up in his eyes.

He choked again for a second and then continued. "I mean, *everyone* kept telling me I was crazy. And it didn't matter how medicated I was at the VA, I just kept being tortured by these dreams! When I got out,

I found out you were going to that party, and I followed you to the parking garage. I thought—maybe if I did set the bomb—my mission from God would be complete, and I wouldn't be plagued by these dreams. I could live out the rest of my life in peace."

After I set the bomb up, I stood in the darkness at the garage and waited for you, thinking that maybe it wouldn't be too late to stop you. Maybe I just needed to get you to understand. Maybe you could help me with the dreams. But then, Elsa ran toward your car, dangling her keys. I didn't know who she was at first, and when I realized she was going to get in, I ran toward her and tried to stop her! But...." Jake gasped and hid his face in his hands. He began whimpering.

As he hid his face, he continued his muffled explanation. "She was just too fast, Doc! I didn't want to kill her. I didn't want to kill *you*, either. I just couldn't stop the dreams! I couldn't sleep. I couldn't live. I couldn't hold down a job. The Army didn't want me. My best friends were dead. My family didn't care about me. Fuck, I'm so sorry.....I killed Elsa and ruined your life and Ariel's life and my life! I know she was a good woman, Doc. I know you miss her, and I know Ariel misses her." Jake was now bawling. "I'm so sorry, Ariel! I know you all hate me!"

Ariel silently watched Jake's confession, as she leaned up against the wall with a glass of orange juice in her hand. Jake's outburst had taken her by surprise. Up until that moment, she failed to understand Joel's desire to involve Jake in blowing up Project Séance at all. She couldn't fathom how

Joel could ever trust the man who murdered his wife. And she didn't believe that Jake seemed to show any remorse for killing Elsa.

Ariel tolerated Jake at Joel's request for patience in the matter. She trusted Joel, and she knew that he wouldn't ask for her participation without good reason. True, in lighter moments, she was entertained by Jake. But she had also been repulsed by him. After all, Elsa was her good friend, and she wasn't sure *she* could ever forgive him for that. She really couldn't comprehend how *Joel* could forgive him for that.

Even after getting to know Jake over the past three days, she didn't realize until now how he had been plagued by such extreme feelings of guilt and remorse regarding his role in Elsa's death. During the time they spent alone, he never permitted himself to discuss anything serious with her, including the events leading to Elsa's death, his tour in Afghanistan, or the seven years he spent in the prison mental hospital.

But Ariel—more than any other person Jake knew—understood that she and Jake were not like other people. She knew how it was to be constantly afflicted by inexplicable dreams. She understood what it was like to be persecuted for being different from everybody else and to never fit in—ever.

She was moved by Jake's sincere emotional outburst. He hadn't permitted her to see this side of himself until now. This was the human side of Jake. He wasn't cutting up or making quick remarks. He was just being a regular guy. And she could now understand how remorseful Jake was for having made such a horrendous mistake, which affected so many people.

As Jake held his face in his hands, whimpering, Joel leaned over and comforted him by patting him on the back. He was glad, in retrospect, that he deleted the email from Timothy McVeigh. Jake was too emotionally labile to read it, and the last thing he probably needed was to be saddled with even more guilt about his past mistakes.

Ariel walked over, with orange juice in hand, and also tried to comfort Jake, who was so overwrought with guilt that his sobs had become almost convulsive. She, in turn, rested her head on Jake's back and sobbed sympathetically. And for several short minutes, Jake, Joel, and Ariel hugged amidst the sounds of uncontrolled weeping. For all, it was a very long-awaited emotional catharsis.

After a few additional minutes of silence, Joel rose, abruptly changed the subject and patted Jake once more on the shoulder. "Okay. Well you guys need to get some rest. Meanwhile, I have a couple of errands to run." Joel informed them, "I'll be back."

Jake wiped off one last sniffle and gazed up. "Oh yeah, Doc? Where you goin'?"

"I've got to take care of some business with my lawyer and the bank. I will be back soon," Joel assured them.

"Well, can you pick up some Waffle House coffee?" Jake requested.

"Sure, I can do that."

When Joel returned several hours later, he had been up all night. He felt emotionally drained, and he was sorely in need of a nap. He carried a large deposit bag and a manila envelope. He made himself a sandwich from the previous night's leftovers, as Jake and Ariel descended the stairs from his bedroom above, half-naked. Jake strutted like a peacock, and Ariel followed, looking extremely guilty.

Joel paused for a minute, knowing full well that they had spent the entire morning having sex. "Aw, man.....I don't want to know anything.....Jeez, I can't believe this. You guys—together—in my bed?"

"Well, Doc. It's December, and it's cold out in the van. Plus, the van's full. If it wasn't, you'd better believe it would have been a rockin'," Jake bragged.

Joel put up his hands. "Please! Don't tell me any more!"

Ariel shrugged her shoulders.

"Aw, crap. Now, I'm tired, and I've gotta go up and change my sheets," Joel complained.

Chapter 34- Assembly of the Bomb

It was already late at night, and Joel had managed to change his sheets and steal a nap. When he awoke, he pulled Ariel aside, handing her the envelope and the bag containing all the remaining cash he had cleaned out of his bank accounts that morning.

"What's this, Joel?"

"It's money for you, Ariel. It's all I have."

"I can't take your money, Joel. You need it, don't you?"

"Sure. But, just in case something happens to me, I want you to keep it. You can use it to start a new life. Use it for whatever you want. Ariel, you're the only person I have to give this to. You were like a daughter to me and Elsa, and I want you to have it."

He handed her the envelope and added, "But here, you've gotta do this one thing for me, if something *does* happen. You need to give this envelope to a man named Pastor Jackson, in trust for a patient of mine named Tunisha Wallis. I set up a fund for her to pay her college tuition in the amount of $250,000. You'll see that she gets it? I mean, if something happens?"

Ariel broke down into tears, hugging him. "Joel, I just have a very bad feeling about this. I know something bad will happen to you."

Hugging her also, Joel patted her on the back. "It's okay. Everything will be as it should be."

At midnight, after they were sure that the brewery was deserted, Joel and Ariel assembled the bomb elements and supplies, as Jake had directed. Joel was quite impressed by Jake's level of bomb making expertise and his acquired knowledge of chemical stoichiometry. Jake mentally walked them through the bomb making process, explaining his instructions for combining the ammonium nitrate and fuel oil mixture, how to align a charge, how to place blasting caps and the Tovex sausage they had acquired. He apologized several times for not having access to military supplies, which would have made the task much easier than it was.

While they worked, Ariel selected some old Beatles tunes to play on the ipod boom box they purchased. Joel felt energized by the music, as he reminisced about his days as a young teenager. Joel, Jake, and Ariel all performed their menial tasks of the evening, moving along with the beat of the music. At times, Jake would interrupt his own instructions with some profound observation about the song playing in the background. "Do you think Paul is really dead? I don't know. I saw his wedding picture, and he kinda looks like it, lately."

Soon returning to the task at hand, Jake cautioned Joel and Ariel about exercising due care in order to safely detonate the bomb. The mission, in this case, was to maximize the destruction of private property while minimizing the loss of human life. He had determined that setting a timer in the building would be too risky, and he employed his expertise in utilizing cell phones in order to detonate the bomb. "That way," he explained, "We can make sure the building and its perimeter are completely clear and set it off at just exactly the right moment. We want to blow up the fuckin' ghosts—not people."

The building, although largely deserted, was not likely to be inhabited at 6 A.M. That was the time they chose to detonate the bomb. Jake had removed the speakers of Joel's cell phone and hooked the phone up to detonate when he called from Priya's phone.

"Okay, it's time," Joel commanded. Immediately, everyone scattered to survey the building's empty rooms to ensure that the building was, indeed, clear of people. Once they were satisfied that no human being remained in close proximity, they moved the van outside the circumference of the projected blast.

On the way out, they noticed that a worker from a nearby warehouse had reported to work early. Jake ran over to him and warned him to steer clear of the building. The worker stubbornly refused to cooperate and leave.

"Look, asshole. There is a fuckin' bomb ready to explode in that building over there. If you value your balls, you had better hold onto them and run for your fuckin' life! Now go!" Jake waved him away, and the scared man drove off.

The three sought cover behind a dumpster on the far side of Cherokee street. Jake knew that they had cleared enough distance between them and the projected blast. He pulled out Priya's phone and hit the speed dial for Joel's number. Nothing happened. He dialed again. Again, nothing happened, and he held Joel's phone up to his ear.

"What is it?" Joel asked.

"Fucking AT&T, man."

"What?"

"I got your goddam voicemail! Shit!" Jake threw down Priya's phone and stomped on it. Then he picked it up and threw it down again, stomping on it repeatedly. "Fuckin' fuck fucker phone!"

Then Jake looked up, hearing sirens in the distance. "Fuck!" he screamed. Then, decidedly he said, "Fuck, that's it. I'm going in! We've got to detonate this thing now. We're out of time." He looked at Ariel, grabbing her and kissing her passionately. "Little lady, you stay here. I'm going in." And he headed off toward the building.

Joel ran after him. "Jake, wait!"

"No, NOW, man!"

In moments, they were back in the brewery. The explosives were assembled, but Joel's cell phone was not receiving a signal. Jake murmured to himself,

265

pulling on wires, cursing and whispering. He seemed oblivious to the humming system Joel and Priya had set in place in the floor above, and even more ignorant of the strange paranormal shadows and lights now surrounding them on the second floor.

"Look, dude. This is our only chance. I've got to detonate this now. If you don't wanna get fuckin' blown away, you need to leave now. You need to get clear of here!"

"Jake, you can't..." Joel pleaded.

Jake stopped for a moment and looked at Joel. "Look, Doc. I've been a wanted man for the past eight years. My best friends are dead. My family doesn't care where I am. I've been a walking corpse since Kandahar, so I might as well be dead. If there's one good thing I can do with my life—if there's a reason why I've managed to survive all these years—it's this. Now go!"

Joel stopped for a brief moment.

"Go!!!" Jake screamed.

"No, Jake. Wait—that's not true. *I've* been the ghost here. *I* died the day Elsa died. But her death wasn't your fault. It was mine. If I'd have listened to you in the very beginning—if I'd have believed you, she would never have been killed. She's the only woman I ever loved, Jake. This is *my* mess, not yours. *I* need to end this."

"But Doc, you can't do this alone."

"Sure I can. You can show me what I need to do."

Joel stopped to think for a brief moment. Then he continued, "Tell me Jake, when you see into the future, what do you see? Do you envision yourself going up in a great explosion with me, or do you see that you still have a future ahead of you? You said that Ariel was the woman of your dreams. Don't you want to be with her?"

Jake considered Dr. Russell's question. "Actually, come to think of it, Doc...I kinda see me and Ariel getting it on and going out to the West Coast to start a band together." Jake smiled.

Joel pleaded earnestly. "Jake, this is all *my* mess. *I* need to be the one to clean it up."

Jake paused to thoughtfully consider what Doctor Russell had been saying to him. Then, he decisively looked up at Joel. "Okay, Doc. I'll show you what you need to do. But we gotta hurry, 'cause they're coming." Within a few seconds, Jake had instructed him on how to properly detonate the bomb.

"I'll give you 45 Mississippis to get your ass clear of here..... one Mississippi....two Mississippi....three Mississippi..." Jake ran down the hallway, down the stairs, out the door, clear of the brewery—as fast as his legs would carry him.

"thirty-five Mississippi—Elsa, baby, if you can hear me, Help me now!!!" Joel cried. "...thirty-six Mississippi, thirty-seven Mississippi..."

Jake had rejoined Ariel behind the dumpster, who greeted him with a tearful and relieved embrace.

By this time, an army of SWAT team vehicles, fire trucks, and City police cars were now pulling up in the distance, blaring their sirens and screeching to a halt at the entrance to the old Lemp Brewery. They were hampered from continuing further by gathering crowds of bystanders, displaced and curious vagrants, and the panicked worker who had been evicted from the building twenty minutes before.

At that moment, an explosion rocked the brewery. A deafening blast ensued, followed by an almost delayed implosion of the brew house. Simultaneously, an asphyxiating billow of smoke and ash rose from the building as it systematically sank to the ground. The sky rained down chunks of mortar and brick on the surrounding streets and those spectators in close proximity.

But the onlookers on Cherokee Street weren't prepared for the onslaught of spirits escaping the blast, as flames consumed the warehouse. First, the crowd shielded themselves from the debris. But they witnessed themselves surrounded by a massive thunder of ghosts and apparitions, lights, and blazing and intense heat. The heat burned so intensely, it seared the hair on their brows and curled whatever foliage remained in proximity as it passed. Some of the bystanders reported that the sound of the explosion was accompanied by deafening screams of anguish, as the blast resounded.

Within a minute, the cacophony had dissipated, and what remained in the wake of the blast was an atmosphere riddled with dust and ash.

Jake shielded an inconsolable Ariel in his arms as Dr. Joel Russell, Project Séance, and the building which formerly housed his laboratory at the old Lemp Brewery were consumed in flames.

The resulting explosion made national news:

It was reported that Doctor Joel Russell, a prominent Saint Louis psychiatrist, and Former U.S. Army Sergeant Jacob Sternen were said to have been killed in a terrorist bombing, which destroyed a major section of the old Lemp Brewery on Cherokee Street. Having been warned of the bomb planted in the brewery, Doctor Russell and Sergeant Sternen heroically cleared the building, minimizing the potential loss of life. Other than those two fatalities, no other person was killed or injured in the explosion. Only portions of Doctor Russell's badly charred remains were discovered, and virtually no trace of Sergeant Sternen's remains were found at the blast site. Memorial services for the two men will be held at a date and location to be disclosed later.

When interviewed about the event, Joanna Watson, former colleague of Doctor Russell's, stated off the record that he had been very depressed since the tragic loss of his wife, Elsa, eight years before. In his fragile emotional state, he had reestablished contact with Jake Sternen, who had managed to "suck Doctor Russell into his delusions". The two had become obsessed with death, established a domain name at www.projectseance.com, and wrote fictitious emails from dead people. Joanna surmised that the two engineered the bomb together, in an elaborate suicide pact.

But she now doubted her initial accusations about Joel's possible involvement in Elsa's death. Part of her wanted to believe that, deep down, Joel was a good man. Although she never understood the exact details of Joel's project, she theorized that his disastrous experiment probably did initially arise from good intentions.

Priya and Raminder had returned to India. If anyone even knew of Priya's involvement, she was now unavailable to corroborate any facts regarding the exact nature of Joel's project.

What Joanna Watson had told the authorities about the deaths of Jake Sternen and Joel Russell was her theory. She convinced herself that the official press release was a lie, but she did nothing to discredit this formal announcement. That was partly because she didn't want to risk her own professional reputation, and partly because Joel had left her his entire interest in the practice in Chesterfield. This included ownership of the entire building and all its contents, which Joel owned free and clear. It also included his interest in the psychiatric partnership that he and Elsa had initially established thirteen years earlier.

Ultimately, the authorities had deemed their official version to be the most appropriate way to report the events leading up to the blast. They felt it was best to protect the public and to preserve the reputations of Doctor Russell, Sergeant Jacob Sternen, the Missouri Department of Health, and the U.S. Army—which would all suffer—if Dr. Watson's suspicions were leaked to the media.

Chapter 35- Epilogue

Within two months, the bombing of the old Lemp Brewery was forgotten. It made national news for the first few nights, but by the end of two weeks, even the Saint Louis local stations weren't talking about it. By the beginning of February, the rubble for the destroyed building and a couple of other abandoned ones at the brewery site, were cleared away. There was no sign that the building had even existed, except for a newly poured concrete foundation used to permanently block off access to the caves below.

Jake Sternen was officially dead, but in reality, he was still very much alive. Even though the U.S. Army chose to declare him a fallen hero, Army Intelligence was fully aware that he was still alive and kicking. However, with support for the war effort waning, combined with U.S. efforts to withdraw troops from Afghanistan, the Army felt that Jake was no longer a threat and the least important of all their pending concerns. They hoped, by clearing his name and reporting him as dead, that he would simply take the hint and disappear for good.

The Army managed to hold a mock memorial service in Jake's honor in upstate New York at his mother's request. This was complete with an Honor Guard. A framed Purple Heart he had earned during his time in the service was placed next to an empty urn. There was no mention of his seven years spent as a prisoner in the state mental institution. Jake, of course, did not attend, but he did threaten to go incognito, just to see who would show up.

Dr. Russell had cleaned out his bank account the day before his death, leaving all his cash and property to Ariel. He requested in his will that Pastor Jackson eulogize him at his memorial service. There were actually many mourners in attendance at Dr. Russell's service, which Jake *did* attend incognito. Some, like Jake, were former patients. Many, like Joanna, were former colleagues. It seemed that, regardless of his difficulties over the past eight years, Joel had been a highly respected and admired member of the Saint Louis community.

Previously homeless, Jake now stayed with Ariel as her live-in boyfriend, trying to slip into his new fictitious identity. The two had plenty of cash, which Joel had left them. And it would be a sufficient amount to comfortably support them for a good fifteen years, if they didn't get carried away with their spending.

Ariel had never returned to work after Joel's death. Both she and Jake were packing up her belongings and life in Saint Louis in order to travel out to California. They had recently started a band together and called it "Emotional Dys-funk-shun". Ariel had hand painted the Ford Transit cargo van in bright colors, sporting the band logo and name in large letters on the side. This was something each of them had always dreamed of. They were writing their own music, and life was good.

In mid-February, Jake and Ariel officially moved out. They had all their gear packed in the cargo van, and she had given away or dumped all her furniture and office clothes in the back alley dumpster. Still, the van was full, and it took all the energy Jake had to pack every last item in so that the load wouldn't come crashing down on their heads when they opened the back doors. That was okay. They just needed to get to L.A., and they could rent a cheap but spacious apartment.

"It's California or bust, baby!" Jake pointed to his tourist shirt and shorts. He dressed for life in California, even though it was only 20 degrees in Saint Louis. Jake put his arms around Ariel, lifting her tiny frame into the air and kissing her. "Damn, we gotta go. It's too fuckin' cold here!"

The two climbed into the van and drove away. Jake rolled down his window and screamed as they drove away. "USB—Play track *On the Road Again*!" As the ipod sync played the bouncing country tune, Jake cried, "Yee ha! Sing it, Willie!"

Of course, Ariel laughed. By this time, she appreciated Jake's vivacity and sense of humor, and she credited Joel for introducing them. She knew he probably had intended for them to get together all along. That is why he came to her house with Jake, enlisting her help. She felt grateful to have known

Joel, who cared enough about her as a friend to help her realize her life's dream making really good music.

But Joel also understood the importance of having someone special to care about. Perhaps it was his final recollection of his love for Elsa which prompted him to play matchmaker for Ariel and Jake. That was how she wanted to remember him. Joel was a man of great insight and talent, who was capable of great compassion.

Ariel and Jake's relationship had progressed to the point where Ariel had introduced Jake to her parents. Her father seemed initially skeptical of Jake's intentions. Jake was, of course, using an assumed name. But aside from this one "minor" deception, he eventually convinced Ariel's father that his intentions were pure. Even though Ariel was about to turn thirty, she was an only child, and her father was naturally still protective of her virtue. On the other hand, Ariel's mother was immediately enchanted by Jake's charm and wit and believed the couple to be perfectly compatible.

After she had made statements to every involved authority regarding the nature and circumstances of Jake and Joel's death, Joanna Watson had grown tired of being bombarded by the flurry of questions from the press. Four weeks after Joel's death, she bought a new cell phone and changed her number. Two weeks after that, she quit the practice and stopped seeing patients altogether. She decided to focus on a new career, serious relationship, and motherhood, since she felt her biological alarm clock had gone off five years earlier.

One day in early spring, Joanna had gone outside in her robe and slippers to get her morning mail. She waved "hello" to her neighbor two doors down, who tended her blooming tulips. She leaned back to reveal a sizeable baby belly, hidden beneath the tie of her very roomy robe. She turned around to take in the beautiful landscape of her own newly purchased house. *This will do nicely,* she thought. *Plenty of friendly neighbors and room for a growing child. Now, all I need is a husband.*

She walked up the stairs to go back into her new home and sat down at her dining room table to read her mail and drink her morning tea. Just as she took her first sip, she received an incoming text message on her brand new cell phone from an unknown number. She read it.

Joanna,

Although I know I never said it during my lifetime, believe that I did love you. I wish you all the happiness in the world.

Time for us both to move on now.

Love, Joel

Joanna wondered about the message and where it came from for just a brief moment. She smiled for a second, reminiscing about what could have been. Then she promptly turned off her cell phone, walked to the kitchen, and dropped it into the trash bin.

L. Lee Starr is a multi-talented writer, publisher, and songwriter, who has lived in Saint Louis, Missouri for the past 14 years. She earned a Bachelor of Arts degree in psychology from the University of South Florida, a Bachelor of Science degree in Clinical Laboratory Science from Barnes-Jewish College of Nursing and Allied Health, and a Bachelor of Health Science degree from the University of Missouri- Saint Louis. She currently works as Medical Laboratory Scientist for Barnes-Jewish Hospital in Saint Louis.

In 1994, she published a musical work of secular recordings entitled *No Secrets* under the pseudonym *A. Pariah*. In 2003, she recorded a CD of original Christian songs entitled *Metamorphosis* under her married name, Lois Prettyman. In addition to her musical interests, she performed in community theatre, informally studied art, designed works of stained glass, and ventured out into making hot glass beads in a profession known as lampwork.

Ms. Starr grew up in rural Connecticut, the daughter of an American father and her Korean mother, who immigrated to the US in 1964. She moved to Avon Park, Florida in 1981 with her father and stepmother, where she met and married her current husband of 28 years, Joe Prettyman. She has one daughter, Ariel, who also lives in Saint Louis.

Séance at the Lemp is her first book with Mystic Hippo Media Publishing. To find out more about her upcoming projects, please log on to www.mystichippo.com.

www.ingramcontent.com/pod-product-compliance
Lightning Source LLC
Chambersburg PA
CBHW020734250626
47155CB00003B/758